CTRL + Z

LESLEY FLOYD

COPYRIGHT © 2022 BY LESLEY FLOYD

Printed by:

Amazon

•

Printed in the United States of America

First Printing Edition, 2022

All rights reserved. This book or parts thereof may not be reproduced in any form, stored in any retrieval system, or transmitted in any form by any means — electronic, mechanical, photocopy, recording, or otherwise — without prior written permission of the publisher, except as provided by United States of America copyright law.

Anthony – Thank you for being the best partner I could ever have on this journey through life. I love you more than you'll ever know and I'm so grateful for the support you've always given me. You support my dreams and passions, and you've supported me in life when I needed it most. I love you the most.

Evelyn – Dream big, baby girl. You can sing or dance or write or operate or litigate or help mommy color her hair one day. Whatever you choose to do, you'll do it well. No matter how grown up you get, you'll always be my little Bear.

To my family and friends – I am thankful for your encouragement as I've branched out in so many ways the last few years. You've all had my back when I needed it and pushed me to reach my goals. You're the real MVPs.

To all the "Zoeys" out there – You know who you are. Remember that you are strong and incredible. Never let anyone make you feel less than, and know that your choices are your own, even when it seems like they're not. You've got this.

Shadow Dynasty Series

BOOK ONE

Your role here is clear. This is the best thing you can do for this small one. You will be saving her from a lifetime of hauntings no child should experience. By accepting this assignment, you will save her. The man, standing still as stone before the Board in an unprecedented face-to-face meeting, slowly nodded his assent.

"I'm always happy to be of service to the Board."

He was dismissed, and the man exited the dark boardroom to the main lobby with fluorescent lights so bright they strained his eyes.

"Can we go now pleeeeease? This place is so bo-riiiinnngg." A nine-year-old girl spoke up from the bench where he'd told her to sit and wait. She was kicking her legs out in front of her and wore a slight pout on her face. As he examined her more closely, he took in her tattered and dirty appearance and marveled at the vibrant personality that shone through despite her tragic circumstances.

Orders are orders.

"Yes, we can leave now. But you must not be so forward with your thoughts. Good children don't speak unless spoken to, and you were supposed to be sitting still.' For good measure, he barked, "Come with me."

For a small moment, she looked like she might cry. He watched as she stood, her eyes down, and walked to meet him. As the two pushed through the main doors, the child took his hand in hers. He should have pulled away but, this one time, he thought her entitled to the one small moment of comfort.

CTRL + Z

DIRECTOR

Why isn't she checking in with us?

"Why isn't she checking in, has something happened with the equipment?"

He glared at the rest of the team, demanding an answer that no one could give him.

Sending her on missions was always hard for him. Not because he didn't think she could do the job- he knew she could. He had spent more than twenty years ensuring she was able to do her job.

But their lives had been entangled for all that time, each one dependent on the other for a variety of reasons. There was no physical or romantic connection. It was simply the nature of the task set out for him by the Board. Because of that, it made him anxious when she was gone. Would she try to run away and leave him- costing him his job and likely his life? How would she survive without him? He was always there for her, in her head on the earpiece, guiding her every step of the way. And she had performed so many missions lately; each one, traveling further and longer. He would have to sabotage her, to keep her close by for a while so he could keep her reigned in, dependent. He usually felt bad for a few moments after a sabotage, but it was for her own good. It was so easy for him to do now, too. Her sense of failure would make her feel weak, remorseful, unwanted. And that would give him ultimate control. But first, he needed to hear her voice, to know she had not abandoned her mission. Or him.

"Someone better run diagnostics and find out why I'm not getting a response. NOW!" He bellowed at the team members, who immediately dispersed around the conference room, either getting on their computers or making calls to their own teams to troubleshoot, all hoping that the issues were someone else's fault.

He sat back down in his chair at the head of the table, eyes on the monitor directly in front of him, waiting for his answer. After about thirty minutes had passed, the communications liaison spoke.

"Sir, all systems are running as expected on our end. No issues with the microphones or audio devices."

The Director nodded slightly, his jaw still set tight, and the communications liaison breathed a sigh of relief.

ZOEY

It was never the waiting that bothered her. It was where she was waiting that tended to invoke anxiety. She could spend hours at a time in a dark, quiet place waiting for her next target to arrive. She could be sitting out in the cold rain or even a rat-infested, abandoned warehouse. Those were simple enough: she could sit there and just *be*. But then there were days like today, when she had to curl up in a small metal trunk and wait to be picked up for transport to her next location. Small spaces *always* got to her. That trapped feeling made her skin crawl, and always left her more on edge during her missions. She had work to do though and feeling trapped in this box was still much better than the alternative if she were to walk away from it, so she waited. "It's been seven hours, Zoey. Did you forget the check-in protocol?" She rolled her eyes as the gentleman's voice came once again through the small earpiece she wore, perfectly obscured by her white hair. He'd been hounding her for a check-in for what seemed like hours, despite knowing she would have nothing to report.

"Check-in. I'm in a box." she whispered through gritted teeth. "Where is the transport?"

"Apparently, it's behind schedule. Looks like five more hours."

Zoey had never given more serious consideration to the idea of spitting out a "bite me" to the Director and abandoning the mission. As she contemplated the consequences, she heard the sounds of the trailer containing her box being connected to a truck and realized that the Director had been toying with her. She didn't take kindly to it and, before she knew it, she was saying the words she'd thought aloud.

"I'm sorry, Zoey, you're inside of a tin can so your voice is a bit muffled. What was that?" His words were dripping with intolerance of her attitude.

"I said, 'check-in, transport in progress.' Sir." Recalcitrance was her best friend in these situations- she'd had years of experience in trying to control her sardonic behavior. Clearly, she had some more work to do.

Another three hours passed, and Zoey's box was deposited at its destination. She quietly checked-in, aware that her target might walk by at any moment. Her training had served her well, as two men and a woman entered the room. Their voices were low, but Zoey had done this enough times to know what they were discussing. The men spoke quickly, discussing the transfer of the "package." Zoey had long ago grown tired of the look of shock on a target's face upon finding out SHE was the package, and so she had worked hard to hone her skills in such a manner that allowed her to do her job before the target ever had time to register her presence.

This time though, she had been cramped in the trunk for far too long. Her body was stiff and ached, and she felt weak, which was unusual for her. When the woman lifted the trunk lid from behind, opening its contents to the two men, Zoey lacked the speed necessary to maneuver out of the box and shoot the tranquilizing darts with which she had been equipped. Instead, the men lifted Zoey from the trunk, each one grasping tightly to one of her arms, her weapon falling to the ground. *I'm never going to hear the end of THIS,* she thought, and sighed aloud. This caught the men off-guard, who gave her a puzzled look before attempting to steer Zoey to a chair in the corner of the room. She allowed her body to go limp, causing the two men's grips to loosen. She kicked her target squarely in the jaw, knocking him to the ground. Then, she grabbed the gun from the floor and perfectly landed her sedating shots on the other man and woman.

"Everything alright, Zoey? Sounds like you're having a tough time there."

This time, she chose not to respond at all.

She moved quickly, dragging the man with the female companion to an adjoining room and sat him up in a chair. She moved the woman next, then returned to see her target starting to stir.

Zoey kicked him back to the ground and placed her foot squarely on his throat. He looked tempted to fight to get away from her but stilled when he realized the tranquilizing gun was pointed directly at him. *Thankfully it looks like a real gun this time.*

Her body ached in protest as she crouched down toward him, but she pushed through the pain and slipped her hand into his inner coat pocket. *What an idiot*, she thought, fishing out a USB drive. *Didn't even try to hide it well.* She grumpily shot him with a tranquilizing dart and sat down on the table beside her. Now that the man and woman in the other room had seen her face, she had to let the Director know. Measures would have to be taken to keep them from talking, but Zoey didn't have the resources nor the permission to take any actions against them other than putting them to sleep.

"Check-in." She took a deep breath before almost whispering, "we have two witnesses."

Silence. Then,

"We'll deploy a *cleanup* team along with your pickup. Get the target back to base."

A pit formed in her stomach at the tone behind that one word. Cleanup. She hadn't needed a cleanup since she was eleven years old. Zoey said nothing else as she placed restraints on the target and readied him to move from the hotel, and she made no eye contact with her pickup team at all.

Zoey sat still as a statue on the plane headed back to headquarters. She was contemplating the just-completed mission. Ideally, she would have snuck out of the chest and fired the tranquilizer darts before anyone in the room had seen her. Now there was the unfortunate possibility that the man or his companion would recall her appearance and begin looking into her, trying to find out who she was and where she was employed. This gave them a lead on looking for the other man, should they find any information about Zoey. Unlikely, but still possible. Her eyes fixed on the man she had captured: restrained and blindfolded at the other end of the cabin. She was angry at him, angry at the mission, and angry at herself. The events played back on a continuous loop in her mind, as she tried to think of ways that she could have positioned herself differently in the trunk or how she could have better paid attention to what was going on in the room; how she could have employed better timing in extricating herself from the cramped space.

The longer the flight went on, the more agitated Zoey became. She glanced at her tactical watch. *12 hours left. Great.* She had never been able to sleep while traveling- plane, train, boat, car. It didn't relax her like it did most other people. Instead, she was always alert. Always watching other people, always staying on guard. By the time she got to her various destinations, she was almost always mentally exhausted from the extreme vigilance. This trip was no exception. Even though most of the people on the plane were on her team, she had no idea whether they had been given orders to detain her. Or worse. And restrained or not, she did not trust her target to not try something. So, when they finally landed and arrived back at headquarters, Zoey was a mixture of angry, edgy, fearful, and weary. What's worse is that she had spent so many years shoving those feelings down, blocking them out, that they overwhelmed her as she made her way through the corridors and, with swift force, she swung her fist wildly.

***

"You'll be replacing that monitor after you spend some time in the detention wing, Agent."

DNP Corp's headquarters, tucked away beneath the surface of picturesque small-town suburbia, had been Zoey's home for as long as she could remember. She had grown accustomed to the sleek interior design, the excessively large-screened monitors, the mazes of hallways that lead to various offices and cells and more hallways. But despite all her years there, and all her experience in the field, she always forgot the most troublesome part of this place she called home- the cameras. Honestly, she knew they were there, but she had become so comfortable with her surroundings in the many years she had lived there that she just didn't pay them much attention. This often got her in trouble and today was no exception. The cameras caught her outburst as she punched a hole right in the middle of one of the large screens. "Zoey!"

The Director's raised voice brought her back into the moment.

"Yes, sir."

Zoey stood motionless and quiet. She knew that she was already on thin ice. He only ever sent her to the detention wing when he was really upset with her, and she knew better than to push his buttons any further at that point.

"You failed your mission."

She opened her mouth to argue, to point out that she had successfully retrieved the drive, detained the target, and delivered him for interrogation, but stopped herself when she saw the look in his eyes. Besides, she knew what he meant. She was considered DNP's best agent for a reason, and her sloppy fieldwork did nothing for her reputation.

"These mistakes can get you killed, Zoey. You've spent the last twenty years here training- more than double the time put in by our more senior agents. You are supposed to be *better*."

The young woman forced herself to keep her gaze focused forward. She *was* better. She'd had more successfully completed missions than most of the other agents combined. And this wasn't a mistake. She hadn't gotten caught trying to speak or peek through a crack in the trunk. Rather, her body had betrayed her, under protest from more than half a day spent pretzeled in a box with no give.

"What am I supposed to do now? When the other agents are all vying for bigger missions and higher-ranking targets, how am I supposed to tell them *you* are the most skilled? No. Maybe it's time to send you back to Camp for retraining."

If he had been trying to bait her, his plan worked. Zoey had no fond memories of Camp, nor did she ever intend to step foot back into the campgrounds.

"Maybe next time YOU should spend a day completely unable to move. If you're able to jump out of the trunk with lightning speed let me know, but I'm willing to bet you'd be begging for aspirin before making it through the first thirty minutes."

Oops.

Twenty years ago, when Zoey was taken in by the Director, she was a child. Maybe that's why she occasionally felt entitled to snap back at him when she didn't like where a situation was going. The look he gave her now made it clear that she possessed no such entitlement.

She thought of apologizing, but knew it was too late. The damage had been done. She might have been able to negotiate the punishment she was about to face, had the Director's field captain not been in the room. But he was, and she knew the crushingly devastating response to come was a show of force.

Examples had to be set. His eyes narrowed and, in a menacing whisper, he spoke.

"Report to the detention wing now. Once medtech has a chance to evaluate the damage you've done to your hand, you'll be moving into a containment cell. You'll have plenty of time to rethink this behavior there."

"Wait, no! I'm sorry! I swear, I'm sorry! It will never happen again!" Zoey's words spilled out quickly, dripping with anxiety. Containment cells were solitary. While she could easily zone out for hours on end waiting for a target, she could not stand being stuck in such a small cell with no indication of date or time, waiting for her *next* punishment. It was like solitary confinement, except with solitary you got to go back to your normal cell and move on with your life. Yeah, you were still locked up, but you weren't isolated, so it was better. Here, something else *always* came after containment. The Director had always been clear about making sure the agents learned their necessary lessons. He wasn't going to take it easy on her just because he had practically acted as a father to her.

"The decision has been made, Zoey. Go, now."

He looked away from her, obviously avoiding the panic in her eyes. He knew what she was thinking and feeling. This was the job though, and someone had to keep her in line. She was far too valuable for DNP to lose to rogue behavior, so he had to stamp it out swiftly.

The field captain placed his hand on Zoey's shoulder, gently enough to not be perceived as a threat while still firm enough to guide her out the door. Zoey walked with him wordlessly, trapped in her own thoughts.

When they arrived at the detention wing, the field captain led Zoey into a small holding cell. A couple other cells also housed agents. Normally, she would have wondered what they had done, but not this time. This time, she began doing everything she could to acclimate herself to her surroundings: day, time, temperature. She would *not* spend weeks in a containment cell without any idea of how much time had passed again. She couldn't.

The medic arrived and began inspecting her hand. Not broken, but a decently deep cut. He elegantly tied quick stitches into her broken skin and bandaged her up.

"It's 6:43 p.m." He whispered to her, as she was summoned out the door and escorted to containment row.

35, 36, 37, 38, 39, 40, 41...

Zoey counted the seconds off in her head. By her calculations, it was around three in the morning, two days after she had first entered the containment cell. Give or take a couple minutes. She sat in the back left corner of the room, focusing solely on how much time was passing. While she knew she wouldn't be able to keep up the count much longer, she held onto hope that she would maintain at least a vague idea of how long she had been confined.

Last time she had been sentenced to containment, they had locked her in for three weeks. Twice a day, at irregular intervals, a small door would open in the wall, providing Zoey with a meal replacement shake. Each shake provided a different calorie and nutrient count, designed to last Zoey until the next one would be provided to her. This time around, she had received five of the shakes so far. They had little to no flavor, but they did the job. It was then that an idea came to her, and she smiled as she finally allowed herself to fall asleep.

Sometime later, Zoey was awoken by continuous bangs on the door. Her meal replacement shake was in the room, and she had slept through its arrival. She smirked and turned over to try to go back to sleep.

"Drink it, Zoey" a voice spoke dryly over the speakers. *Where are the speakers anyway?* She looked around the tiny space and saw nothing. *I'll have to find out how they are pumping the sound inside sometime. Come to think of it, where are the cameras in here? How are they even watching me?*

"Zoey."

"I'm good, thanks!"

She could feel the confusion behind the unidentified voice. After a moment or two passed, the reply came.

"Drink it now, or we'll pull it back out of the room."

"Yeah, I'm really ok so do what you need to do out there."

Another moment passed and then Zoey watched as the drink retracted into the wall and the door closed.

DIRECTOR

"She's doing what?"

"Sir, she's refusing meals. She hasn't taken the last three shakes we've sent to her. She just says she's not hungry and goes back to sleep."

So, she thinks if she goes on a hunger strike, we'll have no choice but to pull her from containment early. Clever, but two can play this game.

"Keep sending them in as scheduled and update me after each one."

He hung up the phone without waiting for a response, knowing his orders would be followed. He seethed as he tried to determine why she would be so recklessly rebellious. She wasn't in charge here. She didn't get to decide what she would or would not do. This brash girl was throwing up a middle finger to her punishment, which meant she was throwing up a middle finger at *him*. He would have to do something about it; he had no choice. Allowing her to be disrespectful when other team members were aware was not an option.

As he made his way to the detention wing where the containment cells were located, he racked his brain trying to figure out what kind of game she was playing. His ward had always been a little reckless, sure, but she wasn't stupid. So, it baffled him that she would take such a risk.

The door to her containment cell slid open, and he saw her lying on the small padding used for beds. She looked so peaceful in her sleep. *Why couldn't she be so serene and quiet all the time?*

"ZOEY!"

The agent sat straight up, looking slightly confused by her sudden waking.

"Is this some sort of game to you, Zoey? You think it's funny to continue to defy me despite your current predicament?"

"What are you talking about?"

"You know full well what I'm talking about, Zoey."

She held his gaze, making it clear to him that she wasn't going to break on this issue.

"Fine, Zoey. We can play this game if that's what you want. We won't be sending anymore drinks in, and I'll come back for you in a few days when it's time to head to Camp. Maybe *that* will help you get a handle on why I might be angry with you."

Whatever he expected to happen next, it wasn't that Zoey would just shrug her shoulders and sit back against the wall. He was so angry that he knelt down beside her and grabbed her chin, yanking her face up to force eye contact with her.

"I will not tolerate your disrespectful attitude; do you understand me?"

"And maybe I won't tolerate being caged up like an animal."

Before he knew it, he had backhanded her so hard that she fell sideways onto her makeshift cot. He immediately regretted the action but was still so enraged that he didn't check on her before storming out of the cell, allowing the door to seal her in once again.

Zoey sat quietly in the window seat in the last row of the business class car on the train; the Director sat immediately to her left. The train hadn't even left the station yet, and she already found herself annoyed by the party of three playing cards in the seats just in front of her.

The Director was clearly unbothered, as he typed away furiously on his laptop without ever stopping to look up. The train hadn't even begun moving yet. Zoey tried to distract herself by staring down at the troves of passengers running up the ramp to catch the train before it stranded them at the station. They had two minutes.

"Last call, last call folks. Please stand clear of the closing doors." The plain and pleasant voice rang throughout the cars.

This is it, she thought. *I could make a run for it right now... He would be stuck on this train for a few hours. That's more than enough time to disappear...*

As if he had read her thoughts, the Director suddenly closed his laptop and placed his left hand on the back of the seat in front of him, turning his body toward Zoey. He had effectively blocked off the option of an easy escape. When he spoke, his voice was low and stern.

"It's not worth it, Zoey. We'll find you, and then this will all be worse for you than it already is." He paused momentarily. "And, you know, you really don't have it that bad here. Yes, you're in trouble. Yes, you hate Camp. But I've given you the opportunity to learn and experience so much more than most people your age. Where do you think you'd be right now if it wasn't for me?"

Zoey turned her head to look out the window as the train started moving forward.

"Answer me, Zoey."

She turned her head back forward, looking down, refusing to rotate to her left. She didn't want to make eye contact when she spoke.

"Dead."

"Yes. A dead child on the cold streets, and no one would have cared. Not even your parents. No, they wanted you to die. They dropped you off in a dark alley and left you because they didn't want you. I found you and brought you in. I went before the Board for you. So perhaps it's time to stop acting out and start acting like the adult you are now. Show some gratitude for your circumstances and do what your told. Do you think *maybe* that might be worth trying?"

"Yes. . ." she was almost inaudible.

Almost menacingly, the Director responded.

"You're going to have to do better than that, Zoey. I can't hear you."

"Yes sir."

"Look at me when you say it, Zoey."
She turned to him, tears forming in her eyes.
"Yes sir."
"Dry it up," he said maliciously, "or you'll spend some more time in containment after we get back from Camp."
Zoey tilted her head downward, closed her eyes, sniffed once, and then looked back at the Director. This time, her eyes were clear, and she wore a blank expression.
"Good, Zoey. Very good."
And then he opened his laptop and went back to work, as if nothing had happened at all.
Zoey didn't have the luxury of distracting herself with work on the train. She presumed that was done on purpose so that she would have to think about what was coming. Again, there was no chance of her getting any sleep-not with so many potential enemies around. Zoey also didn't get the enjoyment others seemed to get at watching the landscapes pass by the train windows. She had never been and would likely never go to any of the places through which they rode, and she'd never been taught to notice the "beauty" of her surroundings. She never understood why they insisted on traveling this way to Camp. They could very easily have gotten into one of DNP's small private planes and flown. At the very least, the Director could have simply had someone drive the two of them in one of the multitudes of black SUVs DNP owned. But instead, they always traveled by train for about seven hours before transitioning to a cargo truck that would drive them another three to

four hours. All in all, it was a very long day of unpleasant travel only to face what was waiting at their final destination.

She stared ahead the cards in the hands of the passenger directly in front of her, wondering how anyone could be so bad at poker. *I guess you don't have to be good at it when there are no stakes.*

That was true though. With everything Zoey did at DNP, the stakes were always high. That's why she was always the best. Being sent back to Camp was an embarrassment. Deep down though, she knew this punishment would have actually ended with a few more days in containment, had she not refused her meals. But she just had to take a stand (against what, she wasn't sure), and now here she was on a train to nowhere for two weeks of remedial agent work. On top of that, she was light-headed and weak. She still hadn't been told how long she'd been in containment, so she didn't know how many days' worth of nutrition she was behind. The Director knew though, and he wasn't offering her anything now, which told her she was really going to regret her act of rebellion during the coming two weeks.

DIRECTOR

Once they arrived at Camp, the Director pointed toward the dormitories and watched as Zoey wordlessly turned and walked toward them. He maintained his gaze on her until she got in the front door, knowing that she'd be getting her room assignment, and then he made for his office. While Camp still had a lot of modern technology and features, it wasn't as elegant as headquarters. As a result, the Director's office was much more cramped. He didn't actually visit very often; only when site visits were an absolute necessity. There was no way he was sending Zoey away for two weeks, though. Not after she'd broken communication while on her last mission. He needed to be able to put eyes on her at any time.

He still couldn't believe the stupidity she'd exhibited in her protest of containment. She was definitely feeling miserable right now. He could see it in the way she'd carried herself across the property to the dorms.

The Director arrived at his miniscule office and unpacked his laptop, connecting it to the secured internet so he could fire off the update to the Board he'd been preparing on the train. They had expressed extreme displeasure at his last report detailing Zoey's belligerence, so he did his best to convey her behavior on the trip as remorseful, even though he wasn't quite sure that was the case. He finalized his proofread, added a few more details, and sent the report. Around that time, the head trainer for the facility walked up to his office door.

"I honestly didn't think you were actually coming with her, Director." He was friendly and gave a small smile. The Director sighed, relaxing back into his leather chair.

"Honestly, this is the last place I want to be, Tom. But she's been so volatile lately that I don't trust her to just do what she's told."

"You want me to give her the typical 'stop screwing up' routine? Get her out for a run in the morning?"

"Let's do an *atypical* 'stop screwing up' routine."

Tom eyed the Director, unclear exactly what he meant. The Director swiveled his chair slightly then continued.

"She's playing games with us, so I want her to see real consequences from that. I don't want her attending meals in the dining hall with everyone. In fact, don't offer her meals period. If she wants to eat, she needs to come to me. And let's double up on the typical routine. Sure, get her out for a run in the morning. But I'd like her doing drills tonight as well. Figure out where your team can pull extra shifts. If they are mad about it, tell them they are welcome to take it out on her. Once you believe she's really broken down, let's put her into an interrogation simulation with the new weapon."

"Sir," Tom started, still unsure whether he wanted to question the Director's commands, "I have no problem giving the double training order, Sir. Or with any of the other orders, really, but-"

"Tread lightly, Tom. I'm in no mood for further insubordination."

The lights almost seemed to flicker in sync with the Director's foul mood.

"No Sir, not insubordination by any means. I just wanted to point out we haven't tested that technology on anyone in interrogation simulations in less than perfect health yet. I wonder if it might be better to do that earlier on, when she has more strength?"

Tom took a slight step back, wanting to place as much distance between himself and the Director as possible without causing further rage.

"No. I want her to have to work hard to pass the tests this time. She's not here for a good time, she's here because she can't follow rules. She needs to understand where that can get her when she is acting out in the field."

The Director could tell Tom wanted to say more but, to his credit, he simply nodded in assent.

"Get her started now, and you have my permission to run drills as late into the night as you wish."

"Yes, sir. We'll make sure she learns her lessons out here, Director." As a method of dismissal, the Director nodded his head and opened his laptop back up, staring at a blank screen.

Yes, she'll learn her lessons. She'll learn that she can't do any of this without me. She can't exist without me. She forfeited all control to me years ago, and she will remember that.

Four days into Camp, and Zoey wasn't sure she was going to survive. The training schedule she'd been put on was worse than any program she'd ever had to endure at Camp, and, because of the late nights and early mornings, she was barely sleeping. She still hadn't eaten anything. There was always water around, but her body was weakening at a dangerous pace. Zoey finally decided, somewhere early in day three, that no one was going to offer her anything or give her permission to go to the dining hall. She was going to have to ask. And while she didn't wholly mind asking Tom, she had a sneaking suspicion that he wasn't the one authorized to give her that permission. Her stunt had been immature, and she knew the Director was furious about it. Still, she felt a burning need to hold onto that control. To not give him the satisfaction of her request for mercy. Especially now that she was enduring these increasingly painful training sessions.

As she gingerly sat in a bathtub full of hot water, she considered her options. What would happen if she simply passed out during one of the next exercises? Sure, they'd take her to medtech, but then what? The thought of extended time at Camp popped into her mind and she immediately resolved to find a way to sneak some food to her dorm so she could get her strength back up without having to admit to anyone that she'd made a terrible mistake. She especially didn't want to admit that to *him*.

After about forty-five minutes had passed and all the water had lost its heat, she resolved herself to stand and get dressed in the required uniform- black athletic pants, black tank top, black sneakers. Not ones for fashion, the trainers in charge. She checked herself briefly in the mirror, opted to leave her wavy white-blonde hair down around her shoulders, and turned to exit the dorm. As she opened the door, there were two guards waiting for her. One made eye contact with her and informed her she'd been ordered to undergo interrogation simulation. Zoey nodded and, as they turned to lead the way, she took a deep breath before following, doing her best to keep her head high.

Of all the things DNP put its agents through at Camp, Zoey hated interrogation simulation the most. She presumed everyone hated it, and that was most likely why names were drawn randomly among those at Camp and participation was mandatory. She also understood the logic behind testing: 1) it was important to know which methods worked and which ones didn't, and 2) DNP Agents were supposed to be able to withstand the most intense interrogation techniques. Secrets were secrets for a reason. As she made her way through the long corridor (escorted by two other agents, per company protocol), she noted the silence around her. Usually there was some noise - a machine humming, someone making small talk, staff members walking by, alarms beeping. But this time, there was no sound at all. She quickly glanced at the two agents flanking her and took in their sober expressions. They knew what was being tested, she realized, and she became keenly aware that they were armed. *To walk me down the hallway?*

Is it so bad they think I'm going to make a run for it? She thought to herself. They should know she wouldn't-not when she was following all of the instructions given to her in an effort not to exacerbate the tenuous situation with the Director. She stopped suddenly and turned to the agent on her right.

"Hey, what exact—"

And then she collapsed to the ground in excruciating pain.

She'd been shot. The agent walking to her left had shot her. *But with what?* This didn't feel like any other gunshot wound she'd had before. Well, it did, but it was different. *What's different?* She tried to focus her thoughts to be prepared for what would come next- the demands for her Agent ID Passcode, a number given to agents each day that they are required to remember, just in case they were selected for testing.

But the pain was too severe for Zoey to perform an accurate analysis. She began to lose consciousness and, quite unnervingly, she heard her own scream of agony before the world around her faded to black.

When Zoey finally awoke, she found herself in very tight four-point restraints on a hospital gurney in an otherwise empty dark room. She pulled at the restraints, testing their tightness. Zoey wasn't going anywhere any time soon.

As she began trying to remember how she'd gotten there, she realized all her pain was gone. *Did they give me painkillers?* But that wouldn't make sense. Why make her feel better right before questioning her? She struggled to place the uniqueness of the pain she had felt but came up with nothing.

"Tell us your Passcode."

A pit formed in Zoey's stomach.

Why is he here? This isn't his job. He's supposed to wait for the report.

"Your Passcode, Zoey."

She felt a chill down her spine as the Director said her name so menacingly. It was then, when she heard a rapidly increasing beeping, that Zoey realized she was hooked to a vitals machine. *This is going to be bad.*

"Zoey. Look at me." The girl turned her head ever so slightly to see the Director, mostly covered in shadows. "We don't have to do this. We can walk away from it now. Just tell me your Passcode and that will be the end of this."

She might not have been sure about what would come next, but Zoey was positive that she would not give her Passcode. At this point, she was the only agent in the company who had passed every test, and she wasn't about to let the Director's presence throw her off her game.

"I don't know what you're talking about." Her words were soft, yet even.

"Zoey. . .please be reasonable."

"I don't know what you're talking about." The only phrase she planned to say until this was over.

"Your Passcode."

"I don't know what you're talking about."

And then, without warning, Zoey felt the white-hot pain of a bullet tearing into her flesh. He hadn't shot her though. Confused, Zoey tried desperately to fight through the pain- the same but unplaceable pain she'd felt before - but she couldn't hold in the screaming. She thrashed ineffectively against her restraints, hoping *anything* she tried would make it cease. She screamed and fought, but the pain was relentless, and this time it was the heart rate alarm system Zoey heard as she succumbed to the darkness.

The pain was gone once again when Zoey began to stir awake. The Director was now sitting in a chair very close to her. Too close for her to hide the tear streaking down her cheek. This time, when he spoke, he whispered so low his voice was almost inaudible.

"What's your Passcode, sweetheart?"

Her heart stopped. He hadn't called her sweetheart since she'd been, what, nine? Ten?

The Director knew what he was doing, of course. That's why he declared that he would be running the test simulation this time. All that time in containment and detention, the lessons on numbing out to all emotions. And now he sought to instill fear in Zoey. He knew she might be able to withstand the pain longer than the simulation had been slated for, but Zoey had not been afraid of anything or anyone in a very long time. Force her to feel a feeling that had been taken from her, and she won't know what to do. She can't act on it, because she doesn't want to get in trouble for letting her emotions get the better of her. The combination of the fear, the anxiety, and the pain. That's what would break her this time.

He leaned in even closer.

"Zoey. Just tell me."

A volleyball-sized lump grew in her throat, and she just managed to croak:

"I don't know what you're talking about."

The Director suddenly stood, knocking his chair backward. Zoey heard something click, and the pain returned. This time, she cried out for help. No one came.

And then, the pain stopped. Just like that, it vanished. *Am I getting stronger and resisting it? It doesn't feel that way...*

"Describe what you feel physically when you're screaming, Zoey." Cold and clinical. She couldn't reconcile his aggressively changing mood, and she was also surprised by the question. The weakened girl allowed her eyes to find his; confusion drawn all over her face. He repeated his order.

"Wha...I don't...what..." She didn't understand but her confusion was clearly not sufficient. The pain swelled up violently and her screams got louder.

The same back-and-forth of searing pain followed by demands of what was unique about the pain went on for days. Or so it seemed- Zoey later found out that this portion of the test ran for about two and a half hours. When she still wasn't able to answer the question, the pain came back and once again lasted until she had passed out.

"Passcode."

Zoey was jolted awake by the harshness of the demand.

"Passcode."

"I don't know what you're talking - -"

Again and again, she lost consciousness. This part continued for another twelve hours.

"TELL ME THE PASSCODE, ZOEY." He roared the words this time, while grasping her tightly at the throat. She heard the click again this time, and she knew she couldn't take it anymore. Just as the pain began rising again, she yelled:

"ZS0427895! ZS0427895! ZS0427895! That's my Passcode, it's ZS0427895!"

And for a moment, the entire world stopped.

DIRECTOR

The medical staff rushed in to attend to her, shooing the Director from the room, glaring at him disapprovingly. The simulation was set to end in about five minutes. The Director had increased the volume on the serum causing Zoey's pain several doses higher than the testing required. He knew that they would likely report him to the Board, but he wasn't all that concerned about retribution. The Board had been growing increasingly concerned about Zoey's rash behavior and slower movements in the field. He knew that this would be the final straw to keep Zoey in line for good, which would keep her safe from the Board for a while longer. And as long as she was under control, he was safe. "Let me know when you've confirmed that she's stable," he said to the doctor over the medical team, who was walking past him to oversee his team.

He then went into his office and closed the door behind him, locking it so he would not be disturbed. Exhausted, he sank into his chair and allowed his thoughts to linger on her screams for just a few moments before dialing into the call set with the Board.

Did she break?

"At the very end." He left it at that. There was no need to disclose the higher dose himself if there was a possibility no one else would report it.

And what happens next?

"She's in medtech now. Then we'll debrief her and explain the weapon we used. Tell her we will require her to repeat the simulation again, and that she'll have to do it successfully before she's allowed to leave Camp. She won't be happy about it, but I'm convinced she will be so terrified of experiencing that again that she will keep her cool and accept it."

Good work today. Remember that it is imperative that we keep her under control. Everything depends on her and her allegiance to us.

ZOEY

"It felt like I had been shot, but not like a normal gunshot wound. Like.... you know how it fades? Your body kind of goes into shock or the bullet settles...it still hurts, but it's not the same as when it's ripping through your flesh and muscle and bone to begin with...it felt like...like that most intensely painful part of being shot without any fading or settling. Just that really high-level excruciating pain."

Zoey sat at the table in the Debriefing Room, her head in her hands, a searing migraine making it hard for her to find the words to describe what she had experienced. An interrogation specialist sat across from her, but she knew they weren't alone. She had noticed the earpiece he wore and wondered exactly who was feeding him questions. Even if it wasn't the Director, she knew he wouldn't be far away. Exhaustion raged through her body.

"I really don't know how else to describe it. It hurt. Worse than any pain I've ever felt before. There's no way anyone here would have outlasted that simulation."

The interrogation specialist opened his mouth to speak but stopped suddenly and cocked his head to the side. Someone was speaking to him. The two sat there silently for a few moments before he spoke.

"If this had happened in an actual mission, disclosing your Passcode could have cost not only your life, but the lives of many others here. Protocol is in place for a reason. Why did you break it?"

"Have they shot you with whatever that was? I wasn't afraid of dying. That pain was unbearable. I did what I did to make it stop. And it wasn't a 'real' scenario. I'm assuming whatever *that* was, it was concocted in a lab here. Is there any evidence at all that any other agency or potential targets possess something even remotely similar?"

DIRECTOR

The Director frowned at his computer. He had expected her to say as little as possible, to not have any fight left in her. Something wasn't right. He called the field captain and demanded that the interrogation specialist leave the room immediately and that all three meet in a nearby conference room. He had to find out why this was unfolding the way it was.

"Get the feed from the simulation. I want to watch the last twenty minutes of it again." He growled out the order. The interrogation specialist jumped from his seat and loaded the scene, displaying it on the large screen on the wall. The interrogation specialist and field captain watched the Director as the Director watched the screen intently. Once it was over, he demanded that they rewind the film and play it again, and again, and again.

"Sir," the field captain almost whispered, "there's nothing out of the ordinary there."

He quickly fell silent under the Director's glare.

"There must be something. Her current behavior doesn't make sense given what just happened. Play it again." He forced the words through barred teeth.

Panic rose inside of him. Had he not just promised the Board that she was completely under control? That he could guarantee her compliance? Why did she still seem... combative?

Then it hit him. She thought it was over. She thought she could go right back to her ridiculous attitude, because there was no way he would put her through that again. He dismissed the field captain, acknowledging that they hadn't missed anything in the video, but he continued watching again and again, resolved to teach Zoey her place.

ZOEY

The agent was half escorted, half carried back to her dorm once the debriefing ended. She wasn't still in physical pain from...whatever that was, but still she was emotionally and physically wrecked. Zoey sank under the covers on her bed, but her thoughts kept her from sleeping despite her absolute weariness.

What was that? How long have they had that weapon, that technology? Did they expect her to use it on targets? Would they start using it against their own agents to maintain order?

If that was their intention, she needed to win back the Director as quickly as possible. She had just begun making plans to seek him out the next time she had the opportunity when she heard a commanding knock on her door. It took multiple attempts to get her voice loud enough for the offer to come inside to become audible. The Director opened the door and stood still for a moment, allowing his eyes to adjust to the darkness. Then he strode silently into her cramped dorm and sat in the small armchair to the right of her bed, flicking on the small lamp on the end table between them. Cocking his head slightly to the side, he raised his eyebrows at her, clearly waiting for her to make the first move.

Zoey tried to raise herself so that she was at least sitting up in the bed, but her body betrayed her, and she was forced to lie on her side, looking up at the Director.

"I think I need something to eat," she rasped.

"Do you?" She could tell from his tone that he wanted his pound of flesh on this one, and she took a steadying breath as she continued.

"I'm feeling pretty weak after this whole week. With the double training sessions and the simulation-"

"Is *that* what made you feel weak? Four days here? Really, Zoey?"

Danger glittered in his eyes as he stared at her.

"I'm...sorry. Okay? I know, I messed up. I just hate containment and it felt like the best option. But I get it, it was stupid." He maintained eye contact without speaking again.

"Please, okay? Please let me eat something." She could feel the desperation seeping out into her voice. The Director must have heard it himself, because he leaned forward, coldness in his features.

"Yes, Zoey. You can eat. But I'm not sure you've really learned how dangerous your little game was. I'll have something brought here to you since you can't even get yourself out of the bed, but from now on, you'll eat what I tell you to eat, when I tell you to eat it. You'll have no input over it whatsoever. And if I hear even the hint of a complaint, you *will* regret it. Is that understood?"

"Yes, sir."

"Good. Get some rest after you eat, you'll be retesting the interrogation simulation in the morning." He got up to exit, not intending to give her time to argue, but turned to address her once more.

"You will learn to obey my orders, Zoey, or DNP may find that you're no longer useful to our work."

She gaped at the door as he left. *He wouldn't terminate me. There's no way, not after everything...* Tears welled in her eyes as she considered the possibility that he might permanently turn on her. The last agent who had been terminated was broken mentally first. As far as Zoey knew, he was still locked in a mental health facility, unlikely to be released any time soon. She even wondered if some agents who were terminated were literally *terminated*. As she contemplated his words, she fought to keep the tears from streaming down her face openly, knowing another agent would be stopping by at some point to deliver whatever meal the Director deemed her worthy of eating. By the time it arrived, it was all she could do to choke it down despite her initial hunger. She did though, aware that the agent who had brought her the meal wouldn't be leaving until he could take an empty tray back to the dining hall.

ZOEY

The remaining ten days of camp passed by mostly uneventfully. Zoey finally managed to withstand the interrogation simulation on her third try. On her final day at Camp, The Director and medical team met with her and explained the interrogation process to her in great detail. She had been shot, but the "bullet" was nothing more than a microchip. It had been designed to latch onto the body's nervous system and release vibrations that create an unbearable amount of pain. The most frightening part of this technology, in Zoey's mind, was that the chip was in her permanently, at least for now. They had proceeded with testing without first making sure they could safely remove the device, and few agents were jumping at the chance to potentially have irreparable nerve damage in a surgical procedure. The team assured her they had no intention of using the device against her, though her quick glance-turned-eye contact with the Director told her he wasn't fully against the idea of keeping her in line with it. Zoey didn't mention it, though, and remained quiet as she listened to the continued discussion.

Once the team finished the explanation and Zoey provided yet another detailed accounting of how the pain felt, whether she could pick out any localized pain, and any other effects it had on her, she stood, intending to head toward her dorm until she was summoned to load up into SUVs.

"Zoey, go to the dining hall and eat, then meet me at the vehicle bay. Thirty minutes."

She turned to look at him, but his eyes were still focused down on a report one of the medical staff had handed him. While she knew she ought to respond with the "yes, sir" she'd been forcing out every day since that first interrogation simulation, she was too annoyed by his implementation of random mealtimes and foods. So instead, she simply turned on her heel and left, going straight to the dining hall. It was around three o'clock in the afternoon, so the area was largely empty. When she made it to the counter one of the staff members looked at her apologetically as he handed her a tray. Grilled chicken breast over a bed of spinach and a glass of water.

Would it really have killed him to at least give me some sort of dressing or seasoning on this?

Zoey took the tray and sat at the closest table, ready to force her way through what she assumed was technically a late lunch. She really had no idea what exactly the Director was up to, but she did know she was always still just a little bit hungry. All she could hope was that he would get bored with this punishment eventually and allow her to return a more normal routine. She refused to ask him about it though, one because she didn't want to give him the satisfaction and two because a part of her was concerned it would only make things worse.

DIRECTOR

A notification on his phone informed the Director that Zoey had followed instructions and would likely be on her way to him at the vehicle bay, where he already sat in an SUV with the privacy panel between him and the driver raised. They would travel this way rather than getting back onto the train- he wouldn't give her the opportunity to take the measly snacks offered by the staff. He knew he was hurting her, weakening her, by drawing out this punishment, but the less strength she had the less she fought back against him. She really hadn't been this obedient since she was very young, and he relished the notion that she was currently completely dependent on him for survival. She couldn't leave without permission he wouldn't grant, and no one would give her food outside of his orders for fear of his wrath. He actually looked forward to his next conversation with the Board.

Movement caught his eye and he saw Zoey walking across the campus toward the car, her arms wrapped around herself. *She looks so weak, so frail. Now is the time to really drive home her current situation.*

He watched her as she got into the vehicle, sitting to his right, and fastening her seatbelt, then knocked on the partition to let the driver know it was time to go. Once they were out on the main roads, he began flipping a small device in the fingers of his right hand, waiting silently for her to notice.

ZOEY

Relieved that she wouldn't be stuck in a cargo van for at least part of the trip, Zoey tried to make herself as comfortable as possible despite the awkward silence between her and the Director. Agents didn't usually get to ride with him, and she wasn't convinced she should be happy about it, but as she didn't want to have to walk back to headquarters, she didn't voice those thoughts.

Is he fidgeting? He hates fidgeting.

She could see the movement in his right hand but did her level best to ignore it, but the constant movement was beginning to irritate her so she turned her head to look, and shock took over. Zoey glanced up at the Director's face then focused back on the object in his hand.

"Something wrong, Zoey?"

She shifted in her seat as best she could with the tightened safety belt as she looked at him. He was holding the small remote that controlled the chip they'd injected into her. *Is he about to use it? Right now? Why would he bring it with him? I have done everything he's told me to do. Is he mad that I didn't acknowledge him when I left the conference room earlier?*

"You and I need to come to an understanding, Zoey. My preference would be to never use this device on you again, but that doesn't mean that I won't. I'm well past the smug attitude, the lack of regard for protocols, and the ease with which you disregard orders. This-" he held up the remote closer to her face, "is my new insurance policy for you. If you make me, I will use it again and again. I'll even use the maximum setting possible. You *will* get in line, Zoey."

For the first time in a very long time, Zoey was afraid of the Director. She knew he meant every word, even though she hadn't realized she'd been on such thin ice for as long as it must have taken him to reach this point. She also knew this meant he would never let her go. Zoey would never earn freedom from DNP, would never get to retire like other agents. She was his prisoner now and forever. That was a hard thought to stomach since she'd always considered him her family. But that was foolish, she realized. He didn't want to be her family any more than her parents had; he just saw more use for her. *Freedom. Where else would I go, anyway, when no one wants me?*

"I'm sorry for my behavior, Director. I'll do better."

He nodded and slipped the remote into the interior breast pocket of his suit and Zoey turned to look out her window, wondering why all of this had happened to her.

ZOEY

Back at headquarters, Zoey was relieved to have the space of her cabin and the opportunity to wear her preferred street clothes. Miraculously, the Director had been giving her some space to relax and reacclimate. He'd even had meals delivered to her room at actual mealtimes, and they had been full meals at that. While she hoped that was a permanent shift, she didn't take it for granted. She'd even made sure she cleaned her plate each time as he'd previously instructed, even when she was full, just to avoid a regression into the deep hunger she'd felt for so long.

She was anxious to get back out of headquarters, to occupy herself with a mission, though she had no expectations that she'd be so lucky. The Director had hardly spoken to her since the ride back from Camp and she'd been trying to keep to herself as much as possible. The less time he was aware of her presence, the less likely she was to accidentally anger him.

Mid-afternoon, Zoey went to the state-of-the-art gym, correctly assuming it would be empty. She was hoping to maintain as much of the endurance and strength she'd gained during the two weeks of grueling training she'd been subjected to, especially now that she had more fuel in her body. She popped in her earbuds, turned her music up as loud as she could, hopped on a treadmill and started an easy pace before cranking the speed up as well.

Her white hair sticking to her sweaty face, she ran as hard as she could for about forty-five minutes before she noticed a figure across the room. The Director had his arms crossed as he leaned back against a wall, watching her. *How long has he been there?*

He didn't make any indication to her that she should come to him, so she returned her focus to her run, bumping up the speed a bit just to show off a little. After she'd hit a full ninety minutes, she slowed the treadmill gradually until she could safely stop, turning her music down some in case he did approach her. The Director was still just watching her so instead of making eye contact or speaking, she went to the weight rack and began a strength routine. Once she'd finished a few reps with lighter weights, she moved to the weight bench, selecting a slightly smaller weight since she didn't have a spotter.

"That seems low, don't you think?"

She started and turned around to see he had snuck up behind her.

"I don't have a spotter, so I-"

"I'm here, aren't I?"

Confused as ever, she nodded slightly and pocketed her earbuds, then wiped some sweat from her brow with the back of her hand before adding more weight to the bar. As she laid down on the bench, she noticed he picked up additional plates and added them to each side of the bar before indicating she should begin. *Another day, another test.* Wordlessly, she began doing reps with the unnecessarily heavy barbell. The Director dutifully helped her reset the bar between sets. By the time she started her fourth set, she was moving much more slowly, her arms aching. Really, she hadn't planned to do more than three sets of the lighter weights, but it was clear to her that the Director wanted her to continue. So, she slowly worked her way through. It was when she shakily began her fifth set that he finally spoke again.

"The Board has set a new target for us, and the team is putting together a strategy. I want you to be the agent in the field, so you'll need to join us for the mission planning session after dinner."

"Where will I be going?" She struggled to get the words out as she put all her effort into raising the bar once more.

"It's a local mission. You'll be returning here when your services aren't needed. We will iron out the details this evening."

"Okay." She spoke through gritted teeth, forcing herself to work through the last two reps rather than giving up. As she raised the bar for a final time, the Director paused.

"I don't believe that's the answer I was looking for, Zoey."

She could feel herself losing her grip, knowing she was seconds from dropping the bar on her chest.

"I meant yes, sir."

Another moment passed before he helped her set the bar once more, and her arms twitched from the strain of holding the weight.

"7:30, conference room A."

"Yes, sir."

"It might not be a bad idea to get a few more miles in, just to make sure you're on your A-game." He angled his chin in the direction of the treadmill, focused his eyes back on Zoey, then left the gym. The last thing she wanted to do was more running, but she knew he would check the cameras later, so she begrudgingly got back on the treadmill and ran another four miles. Afterward, she went straight to her cabin and took a long, hot shower before climbing into her bed until dinner was delivered to her room at 7. Chicken and spinach again.

ZOEY

Mission planning sessions could be tiresome, but they were a necessary part of the job. If she'd had her way, Zoey would plot out her missions on her own and conduct them alone- much less likelihood of getting caught if you didn't have to move multiple people through a zone or speak to anyone. But going alone wasn't an option, and neither was doing things your own way. Rules of engagement and all that. So, Zoey sat in the conference room with the Director, the field captain, the coordinator, and the head of weapons management, trying to stay focused on the discussion.

"Our target is Todd Maxwell. He's a forty-seven-year-old President at Mirror Bank. Wife, four kids- three boys and one girl. Mr. Maxwell has been conducting some high dollar transactions lately and with some very interesting clients. Zoey, we need you to get close to Mr. Maxwell and find out who his business associates work for, the purpose of the transfers, and whether someone else is pulling his strings." Zoey blinked at the coordinator.

"Isn't this more of an…. entry level mission? I'm not…over-qualified?"

The Director looked up from his monitor and made eye contact with Zoey.

"I mean, I'm not refusing to do it and I'm not trying to be difficult...I just haven't had this kind of assignment in a long time..."

"And so maybe you're just the right person for this one, Zoey." The Director's tone was harsh. "After all, you don't want to sacrifice your more *basic* skills by focusing on only one line of work."

Zoey nodded. Reading between the lines, she knew that she was still being punished for her previous mission errors, and she had no desire to go back into containment. His power play had worked-she intended nothing short of full obedience going forward.

"Anyway," the coordinator continued, "we'll need to work on a cover for you."

"Surely he needs a personal assistant?" The field captain spoke up suddenly.

The coordinator shook her head. "He's had the same assistant for the last ten years. There's no way we are getting a new one in and establishing a close enough relationship."

"An intern?"

"Mirror Bank does not have an intern policy in place."

"What about his wife?" Zoey interjected.

The coordinator rounded on her. "I don't think we're going to convince him that *you* are his wife, Zoey."

"Obviously." Zoey couldn't hide the irritation in her voice and chose not to look at her boss for fear of antagonizing him. "This report you've given us says that Mrs. Maxwell is an Assistant Vice President at Mirror Bank. Her secretary quit six months ago, and she's been using a temp service since then. If I could go in as *her* personal assistant, I'd still have access to all of the bank, and I'd still be able to get close to them as a couple. Could probably even make friends with Mr. Maxwell's assistant, too. I bet she has a lot of stories."

The Director barely hid a smirk. "Zoey relegated to running errands for an entitled, self-important woman with too much money on her hands. I can't wait to see this."

She had to work incredibly hard not to roll her eyes. "I've had worse covers. What are your thoughts, Trev?"

Trevor never looked up from his sketchpad. "Well, if you're going to be spending a lot of time in a bank, you can't have any obvious weapons. I'm not sure that you will need anything major anyway, considering this is an information-gathering mission. But I think we can definitely get you some goodies dressed up as makeup items."

"I don't want her to be unarmed, Trevor." The Director cautioned. "She might be there to gather information, but if she gets caught and we don't yet know what exactly is going on, she doesn't need to be handicapped any more than the cover already makes her."

Trevor nodded. "I'll make sure we can fit a weapon into an item Zoey might carry as a personal assistant."

"Alright. Let's get Zoey a new name and an interview with Jemma Maxwell."

And with that, everyone knew the meeting was over and that they had been dismissed.

"Come with me, Zoey. We'll get your identity configured." The coordinator stood at the door waiting for Zoey to follow her through.

ZOEY

"Hello, my name is Katie Charles. I have an interview with Mrs. Maxwell at 2:00? I'm a bit early…"

Edna, the elderly lady at the front desk, looked up at Zoey and smiled.

"Yes, of course, darling. Mrs. Maxwell is wrapping up a meeting now but will be with you right at 2. She's never late, that one. Would you like some water or coffee while you wait?"

"Oh, no ma'am, thank you though. That's very kind of you." Zoey flashed a timid smile.

"Okay darling, well you just go sit over there in one of those big ol' chairs and make yourself right at home. And if you need anything at all you just come let me know."

"Yes ma'am, thank you!"

Zoey walked over to the chairs, looking at her surroundings in a feigned sense of wonder. She knew Mrs. Maxwell would expect her to be impressed by the offices, but not starstruck. She finally selected a chair and sat on the edge of it, back straight as could be, rather than sinking in for maximum comfort. "Ms. Charles?" A tall, muscularly built woman with the shiniest black hair Zoey had ever seen was standing next to Edna.

"Oh, um, yes ma'am, you can call me Katie, please, ma'am." Zoey stumbled over the words as she fumbled out of her chair. *Gotta seem a little nervous.*

"Of course, Katie. I'm Jemma Maxwell." She elegantly extended her hand to Zoey, who timidly shook it. "If you're ready, why don't you come with me, and we can get started."

Zoey nodded her head and followed Jemma through a maze of a hallway, all quiet except for the echoing of their heels on the grand marble floor. They entered Jemma's office. Jemma motioned for Zoey to sit, and she sat opposite Zoey in the other guest chair.

Interesting. I would've pegged her for a 'sitting at the desk, I'm in charge here' type of interviewer. Zoey was glad no one at headquarters could hear her thoughts- it was much too early to be reading any of the people wrong.

"I must say, Katie, I found your resume to be quite intriguing. Fluent in several languages, a robust history as a paralegal, and the former personal aide to Helen Storms over at Catalyst Computing. This position seems like it would be too...low-key for you."

Zoey gave a soft smile.

"Well, Mrs. Maxwell, I don't believe that working for you would be low-key at all. In fact, I've been following you in all of the 'Most Powerful Women' magazines and articles and, to be quite honest, I think I could learn a lot from you. Not that I'm expecting you to be a mentor to me—" Zoey rushed to get the words out, "it's just that I know that powerful people surround themselves with powerful people. I haven't been out of college for very long but, as you noted, I do have an impressive resume. And in order to make the decisions for my long-term career goals, I need to see how it's done by people who know what they are doing. And for that, I'm happy to assist you in any of your needs."

Jemma relaxed more in her chair.

"Very complimentary of you, Katie. And also bold, to tell your prospective employer that you want to work for her just to use her." She held a hand up as Zoey opened her mouth to speak again, to correct her overconfidence, "I'm not offended by it. In fact, I value it. I prefer to know what I'm getting rather than be blindsided by it.

I'm very demanding, though. I want what I want when I say I want it. I have no tolerance for mistakes with my calendar, and confidentiality is of the utmost importance here. I'm also not looking for an assistant who isn't willing to work outside of the nine-to-five life. I work at all hours and am looking for someone who is willing and able to do the same."

"I'm happy to be at your beck and call, Mrs. Maxwell. So long as I'm paid appropriately for it." This time, Zoey relaxed back into her seat, making it clear that she was not as meek as she'd portrayed to Edna. Jemma grinned.

"I think you'll find your pay to be more than sufficient, Katie. How soon could you start?" She stood and walked to her desk.

"Whenever you'd like, Mrs. Maxwell."

"Wonderful." She dropped a large, heavy banker's box into Zoey's lap. I need everything in this box copied. Bring the originals back here, then redact the copies- no names, social security numbers, addresses: basically, no identifying information. Then I'll need ten more copies, placed into three-ring binders, with dividers between each section. There are pages in the stack in this box indicating those sections. It's time to get to work, Katie."

Zoey smiled at Jemma and strolled back through the corridor to Edna's desk. "Is there any chance at all you could point me toward the copy room, please?"

Edna gave Zoey almost a sad smile, placed her "I'll be back soon" sign on the top of her desk, and escorted Zoey away.

ZOEY

Zoey spent the next six hours performing various tasks for Jemma. Finally, at 8:00 pm, Jemma told her to go home for the evening and get some rest- Jemma had a phone conference with some international contacts at 5:00 am the next morning, and so she needed Zoey to be at the office by 4:30 am. As Zoey was leaving, Jemma called out her morning coffee order to Zoey, knowing full-well that none of the coffee shops in the area would open before Zoey's required arrival time.

She climbed into the ten-year-old economy sedan she'd been given as part of her cover and dialed into headquarters.

"I'm on my way back." She said shortly and disconnected before she could be transferred for any preemptive questions. She'd hoped that a full debriefing wouldn't be necessary, but those hopes were quickly dashed. The coordinator was waiting for her when she walked in the main doors and the two returned to the conference room where the mission had been planned. Trevor wasn't there, but the field captain and the Director were waiting in their usual seats. Zoey repeated every bit of information she could recall from the papers in the box five times before the coordinator changed the subject.

"What can you tell me about Edna?" The coordinator asked.

Zoey looked at the coordinator as if he had lost his mind.

"Edna?" She repeated, giving him the opportunity to move on from that subject.

"Yes, Edna. I want to know everything there is to know about her."

She was too tired for this and looked to the Director for help.

"Zoey, you've been asked to describe a bank employee. Please do so." He half raised an eyebrow as if he were daring her to argue.

"Edna is... Edna. She's in her mid-seventies and could have retired years ago, but she doesn't have anyone at home and the bank treats her well, so she stays. She doesn't do much other than greet people who come inside. I didn't really spend much time around her. I waited in a chair by her until Jemma came for me. Then I asked her to show me where the copy room was, which she did. That's it."

The Director's gaze was still fixed on Zoey.

"When you asked her to take you to the copy room, what did she say? How did she act?"

"She said. . .she said 'of course, sweetie,' and then she put her sign on her desk and told me to follow her. She acted like; I don't know. . .like someone's grandmother. Maybe she looked a little tired."

The Director nodded as the coordinator scribbled furiously onto a notepad Finally, the Director ended the debriefing and ordered her to bed.

"You'll need to be alert in order to glean details from this call. It's doubtful that she'll let you listen in on it, so you're going to have to be on top of your game."

He then gestured toward the door. Zoey *hated* when he implemented "lights-out" policies. She was thirty years old and perfectly aware of how much sleep she needed to be truly effective at her work. At times she'd ignored the orders, but that always ended in trouble for her, which she was still keen to avoid. So, she walked slowly through the corridors to the residential wing.

Very few agents lived on campus. A handful of them lived in the neighborhood above-ground, and the rest were scattered around the country. The Director, field captain, coordinator, and Trevor all lived on campus, as well as most of the support staff. The only other agents who lived there, though, were Henson, a fifty-two-year-old who'd been shot in the side on his last mission and needed pretty regular medical treatment for resulting conditions, and Shawn. Shawn was just two years older than Zoey, and the two were incapable of getting along with each other. He wanted to prove *he* was the best agent they had. Zoey wanted to punch him in the face. She did, once, and spent three weeks in containment for it. You've got to stop feeling emotions, Zoey. They'll get you killed; the Director had explained. Agents weren't trained to have feelings; they were trained to lack them.

Fortunately, no one was around as she made her way to her cabin. Everyone's cabin was the same size and layout, except for the Director's. Zoey knew he had a much bigger living space, but she had never been inside. Cabins were the one ounce of privacy anyone got at headquarters, and that privacy was guarded definitively.

The exception to uniformity with the cookie-cutter cabins was design. Agents and staff were given free rein to decorate their cabins as they saw fit. When Zoey first moved into headquarters, her cabin stayed bare. She was too young to care much for design and she preferred not to be cooped up all day anyway. Now, her cabin was where she preferred to be- alone, but with the ability to read or sketch.

She entered her cabin through the main door, which opened up into a large room with a concrete floor. Directly ahead of her, on a wall opposite where she stood, was her bed. To the right, a small couch and a television sitting atop a grey dresser. To her left, in a small nook just past the door, sat a bistro table with two chairs. Both the left and right walls housed decently sized closets.

On either side of the bed were openings in the wall- not small enough to be doorways, but not large enough to make the space open. Crossing through landed you in the kitchen- small, but sufficient. Her bathroom was behind a door to the left. There was a pull-down ladder in the kitchen ceiling that led to a small loft. Zoey assumed some of her neighbors might have placed their beds up there, but the space wasn't quite tall enough to stand all the way. She got enough of small spaces as it was and had no desire to force herself to sleep in one every night. Instead, she used the area for additional storage. In reality, this meant there was a box of old toys from her childhood and a box of old schoolbooks up there, and nothing more. She had never really owned very much in the way of stuff. As far as design, Zoey had left the walls white but hung colorful art along the walls. Everything was modern and sleek, and she kept her cabin spotless.

After a quick shower, Zoey got in bed. She knew that the band on her wrist, designed to look like an ordinary smart watch, was transmitting vitals to the Watchers. Watchers were the agents who enforced orders on behalf of the Director. If she didn't go to sleep soon, one of them would most certainly let him know.

ZOEY

"Good morning, Agent Z. This is your 0300 wake up call. 0300. Please see the Director on your way out."

The cheerful AI voice of a British robot rushed into the room what seemed like mere seconds after Zoey had fallen asleep. This was typical during assignments. The planning team would ensure that the agent was awake with enough time to arrive at the targeted location by programming the location into the system, along with the time the agent needed to arrive. The system would then calculate how long the agent would need to get ready and set the wake-up call accordingly. Likewise, if any additional instructions were given (like meeting with the Director before leaving the grounds), those would be calculated as well. Zoey remained in bed for another fifteen minutes before the voice returned.

"Agent Z, you're going to be late if you do not leave in the next twenty minutes. Please get ready now."

Groaning in frustration, Zoey got up and walked to the closet on the same side of the room as her sofa and couch and placed her palm on the monitor hidden on the back wall.

"Good morning, Agent Z. Your clothing for today has been delivered to your door. Someone will meet you with the coffee Mrs. Maxwell has requested on your way out."

After retrieving her clothing from the hallway - a fitted navy blue dress with dark brown heels and matching handbag, Zoey went to the kitchen. Uninterested in the menu suggestion, Zoey decided she would wait and eat later. She got dressed and left the cabin, on her way to meet the Director.

They always met in the same location when he wanted to see her before a mission. There was a small courtyard with a water fountain in the neighborhood above ground. Six small benches rounded the outside ring of the stone fixture. As Zoey walked over to sit beside him, she noticed that he looked more tired than she had ever seen. Weary and almost…worn. This morning, he looked more like one of the "regulars" that lived in the quaint area than he did a powerful commander. She sat beside him and waited for him to speak. "I know you believe this mission is beneath you," he spoke gently, his eyes locked on the fountain, "but it's much more dangerous than you realize. There are a lot of moving parts on this one, and a lot of different people involved. It's imperative that you keep your focus. Pay attention to everything; remember everything. Always be alert. Follow the check-in protocols. This mission has to be successful."

Zoey took her eyes off the fountain and turned to look at the Director.

"I get it. Besides, aren't they all supposed to be successful?"

Still not looking at her, he replied: "This one is different, Zoey. Please, stay focused."

With that, he stood and made his way to the red brick house about a hundred feet to his right. The stairs to the basement would lead him directly back to his cabin area.

Unnerved by his demeanor, Zoey sat still for a few more moments before making her way to the house with yellow vinyl siding two blocks over. This one would deposit her in the garage, where a staff member was waiting for Zoey with car keys and two cups of coffee.

DIRECTOR

Once he had entered the house and closed the door, the Director stood motionless as he watched Zoey through a window. He always waited and watched after one of these meetings. The first time was out of pure curiosity. He had wanted to know if he could see any sort of reaction. That time, Zoey had stood on the ledge of the fountain and walked its circumference a few times before hopping down and walking away. The next time, he realized she had brought pennies with her and was tossing them one at a time into the water. Sometimes, she just sat quietly while other times she paced, as if she was replaying their meeting in her mind. This time, Zoey sat still on the bench. Reflecting on their conversation, he hoped. He knew Zoey was drastically underestimating how dangerous this mission truly was. The Board had forced the Director into the life of Todd Maxwell some time ago, but he had not been authorized to share that information with anyone else at DNP, especially not Zoey. Pleading with her to take the operation seriously was the best he could do. He hoped it was enough.

CTRL + Z

After Zoey had walked off and disappeared around the block, he made his way to the door that led to the basement and walked down the stairs.

ZOEY

Jemma Maxwell looked stunned when Zoey walked in and presented her with a piping hot cup of her favorite coffee. She'd wanted Zoey to panic over not being able to find it anywhere, to come into work remorseful in hopes that it might knock Zoey's confidence down just a tad.

"Thank you, Katie…I…appreciate it. You must be very…resourceful."

"Like I said yesterday, Mrs. Maxwell. I'm here to do a job, and I'm the best at what I do."

She flashed a smile at her new employer.

"Now, is there anything else you need before the call gets started? I can move all these binders out of your way."

Zoey reached for the stack of binders containing the copies she had made and organized the day before and, without Jemma noticing, stuck a very small microphone to the bottom of the desk. They could make them in the form of stickers now-flat and transparent. "No Katie, that won't be necessary." She brushed Zoey away. "I prefer if you don't touch anything on my desk for now. I manage a lot of very sensitive information and we've only just started getting to know each other."

"My apologies, Mrs. Maxwell."

"It's fine, Katie. Why don't you get started on a translation project for me? I'll need it handwritten-it's too sensitive to be stored in the computers right now. The files are in a conference room down the hall and on the right. They'll need to be translated from Croatian."

Croatian. *Okay. Not one of the languages I speak. Fantastic.*

When Zoey arrived at the conference room, she counted forty-five banker boxes full of papers. As she was just trying to determine where to start, the phone in the conference room rang. Jemma's name appeared on the caller ID.

"Yes, Mrs. Maxwell?"

"I forgot to mention Katie, I'll need those finalized translations by noon on Friday."

ZOEY

Zoey sat at the table with a stack of the papers, a notepad, and a pen. She subtly reached up and adjusted her clear earpiece.

"Any chance one of you guys is fluent in Croatian? I've got a bit of a deadline."

"I told you that you'd regret dropping out of the language curriculum early."

"I am having a lot of regrets right now and none of them involve quitting after learning seven languages. There are a lot of boxes in here."

"Show us what we're looking at so we can assess."

Zoey fished a pair of glasses out of her handbag and put them on her face. A faint grid appeared in her line of sight and a transmission of what she could see was uploaded to DNP's computers.

"Okay...standby, we'll get someone from Linguistics online to dictate translations to you. Will you be able to let anyone into the bank after Jemma leaves?"

"Not without walking by about four cameras."

"We'll figure it out."

Zoey leaned back in a chair and drummed her fingers on the table as she contemplated the volumes of documentation.

"Alright Zoey. We need you to pick up each page, one at a time, and give us a clear look at it. We'll scan the images into our database through your glasses. That will let us look for any buried evidence of criminal activity while also translating for us. We'll have someone in transcription simultaneously write out the translations for you to bring back to work by the deadline, if not sooner."

How exciting, she thought but didn't speak for fear of being told she would have to handwrite the transcriptions instead.

"Jemma's call is starting, sir." Another voice interrupted. The Director ordered that the call be patched through both their intercoms and Zoey's earpiece while Zoey made her way through the boxes.

"It's lovely to speak to you again, Mrs. Maxwell."

"Oh Thomas, I've told you to call me Jemma."

"Of course, Jemma."

"What is our current status?"

"Well, Mrs. Maxwe—Jemma, we are still on schedule right now. There was a slight hiccup with securing a delivery team, but Karl was able to find a replacement quickly enough that we should experience no problems on that front."

"What kind of hiccup, exactly?" Jemma sounded concerned.

"A member of the original crew was picked up on some unrelated drug charges, that's all. We wanted to avoid using a team with any unnecessary legal attention, so we decided to go in a different direction. Nothing that you should be worried about right now at all."

"I'm worried about everything, Thomas. That's the only way this stands a chance of being successful. How much extra is the new delivery team charging us?"

"We got them to agree to the same price, ma'am."

Jemma audibly sighed.

"What else, Thomas? What aren't you telling me?"

"Nothing, Jemma. We just need to know where the pickup and delivery will be."

"I'm working on the translations as we speak."

"Hey while we're on the phone, any chance you could bump up the amount of interest I'm earning on my savings account with you guys? I could use- —"

Jemma hung up on Thomas before he could finish his sentence.

"Alright team, let's find out who Thomas is, and see if we can run down a local drug charge on someone hopefully tied to previous getaways." The Director's voice came through Zoey's earpiece.

"Sir, I hate to be the bearer of bad news but the likelihood of us finding the original delivery team through a drug charge is pretty slim..."

"DO IT," the Director barked at the field manager. "Zoey, get through those documents and get back to base so we can figure out our next steps."

"Aye, aye Captain," she muttered softly.

"What?" He rounded on her.

"I said yes, sir." She held her hands in the air to indicate surrender.

Eight hours later, Zoey had finally finished working her way through all forty-five boxes. Fortunately, some pages had significantly less information on them than others, but it was going to take a very long time to analyze all the information once translated. Once the last page was tucked neatly back into place, Zoey stood, turned off the lights, and walked down the hallway. Jemma had already left for the day. Zoey exited and got into her car, removing both her glasses and earpiece. She needed a few moments of peace and quiet before getting back to the team.

DIRECTOR

"Why isn't she responding??"

"It seems like she removed her earpiece sir. I'm sure she'll be back shortly. We did see her get into her car."

Hell to pay. Absolutely. He was sick of her disconnecting herself from him, as if their connection was her choice. It most certainly was not. He would not tolerate her shutting him out, ever. He stormed from the conference room back to his office and pulled up the security camera for the parking entrance, waiting impatiently for Zoey to arrive.

ZOEY

Once Zoey had gotten a few blocks away from the bank, she pulled over into an empty parking lot. She knew she was supposed to go straight back, but she just needed a moment to breathe. To be alone. No voices, no documents, no other people. She cracked her windows slightly and shut off the engine, then leaned her seat back to relax. Relax. What a strange concept, she thought. She allowed all thoughts of work, of base, of the Director to leave her mind as she reclined and watched the evening sky. And then, she dozed into one of the most restful sleeps she'd had in years.

Two hours later, she woke up with a start. *Oh no*, she groaned. She'd meant to only sit for 5-10 minutes. An unexplained, unauthorized two-hour delay was not going to go over well. Zoey sat her chair up and looked in the mirror, noting that she *looked* like she had been sleeping for days. She lightly slapped her cheeks to wake herself up more, cranked the engine, and sped out of the parking lot.

The sounds of sirens coupled with flashing blue lights disoriented her.

You've GOT to be kidding me.

Zoey pulled over just a short way down and waited for the office.

"Name?"

"Katie Charles," she spoke as politely as she could muster.

"Can I see your license, Ms. Charles?"

She quickly fished the license out and handed it to the officer.

"Do you know why I pulled you over Ms. Charles?"

"Actually, no sir, I'm not sure. Was there a red light I missed?"

"You're going 65 in a 40, ma'am."

"What? Oh my gosh. I'm so sorry, I didn't realize I was going that fast! I was just trying to get home. I'm really sorry!"

"Wait here."

The officer walked back to his car.

I'm never going to hear the end of this...

After a few moments, the officer returned with her license.

"You don't have any tickets on your record so I'm going to let you off with a warning this time. Slow down, Ms. Charles. You're going to hurt yourself or someone else."

She thanked him profusely, innocently smiling at him. Once he was gone, she breathed a sigh of relief. *At least I don't have to take a ticket back with me...*

DIRECTOR

"You can NOT just disappear for hours at a time during an assignment, Zoey! The whole point of check-ins and strict schedules is to keep you safe. How could you possibly be so reckless?"

The Director had been yelling at everyone in sight since Zoey's arrival had first been delayed, and he had no intention of calming down any time soon. He kept his eyes fixed on the errant agent, who at least looked slightly remorseful. He supposed she would apologize, but he wasn't ready to give her the opportunity.

"AND you just got yourself OUT of trouble here. Do you just enjoy getting sent back to Camp? If you weren't already so embedded in this mission, I'd put you back in containment for the next year!"

She hid it well, but he still noticed the almost imperceptible shiver she tried to suppress.

A gentle knock on the door made him snap. "What?" he demanded.

Trevor walked in, giving Zoey an almost sympathetic look just before producing a small case to the Director, who spoke in a lower voice for the first time in hours.

"Zoey. Trevor's going to inject a GPS tracker into your shoulder. If you go through any scans at work, we will be able to momentarily deactivate it on our end. Otherwise, we will know exactly where you are and how to find you from now on."

I will know. I have to know.

The agent looked like she was just about to protest but stopped when she saw the look in his eyes. He knew how to look at her, how to control her. Zoey placed her arms on the table in front of her and leaned forward, giving Trevor the angle he needed to inject the tracker.

Now. Now I will always know.

ZOEY

Zoey sat on her bed, stretching her neck. She could still feel the sting from the GPS implantation and, even though the device itself was miniscule, she believed she could feel it below her skin. She was hurt that the Director had ordered it. The only freedom she ever had in her entire life was the occasional short burst of time between a mission and heading back to base. It's where she could dream of a different life, running away to start one where her every moment wasn't micromanaged. He had taken that away from her. As long as this device was in her body and was active, she would never have any hope at any freedom, though she never really intended to run in the first place. With this device, he told her he no longer trusted her in any capacity, and she ached at the thought of losing his faith in her. Even at her most rebellious, he was the only family she'd ever had, and she never wanted to risk losing the one person who occasionally acted as if he cared about her.

Two devices, no bigger than a millimeter or two each, and she would never be able to leave DNP. While she wasn't in a hurry necessarily, she really had hoped she could retire one day. Going and living on a beach seemed cheesy, but she was sure she could find *somewhere* to go, far away from orders and training and traveling in tiny boxes. That's how she had continued to push through the last few years. DNP had been great to her; the Director had been great to her. She would forever be grateful for that. But as she got older, she longed for a chance at normalcy more often than she wanted to admit. Now, even if he let her go one day, she still wouldn't be completely free of his control. He could always find her, always hurt her, always force her compliance.

Wanting to ignore the hurt she technically wasn't allowed to feel in the first place, Zoey ignored the lights out warning from her room's AI and reached for her sketchbook instead, drawing a girl overlooking a city from a hill, her blonde hair billowing in the wind, darkness behind her.

ZOEY

Early Friday morning, Zoey arrived at the bank before everyone except Edna, who gave her a smile and offered her a piece of candy. Zoey politely declined, asked Edna to tell Jemma where she would be, and made her way back to the conference room. There, she began pulling the last of the handwritten transcriptions of the documents Jemma had requested from her purse, her backpack, and the interior lining of her coat. She'd been sneaking them in this way all week, and she hoped that if she had them ready for Jemma as soon as she arrived, Jemma might let her sit in on some of the meetings on her calendar.

There were three meetings before noon, to be exact, along with a notation that she needed to speak with Todd at 1. Zoey found that slightly odd, as she hadn't seen Jemma schedule time with her husband any other day that week, but assumed they were likely planning to make sure that they would both have their work wrapped up in time for them to take their weekend getaway.

Zoey pulled together her full stack of transcriptions and placed them neatly on the conference room table. A movement caught her eye, and she looked up just as Todd Maxwell walked past the conference room. He didn't acknowledge her there, but he never did acknowledge her when she'd seen him in the past. She wondered if was simply trying to avoid accusations of unfaithfulness by ignoring basically every woman working in the office, but it didn't really matter. The less he noticed her, the better.

"So, you finished the project with a couple hours to spare. I'm impressed." And she did look at least slightly impressed, before donning a slight frown.

"Katie, remind me how you found out about this position originally. I was thinking about it this morning, and I don't believe I ever put an advertisement out for it."

"Oh, well I actually am friends with a girl at the temp agency you were using. She mentioned it in passing, and I just decided to send my resume along."

"I see. What's your friend's name?"

I hope someone on the other end of this earpiece is digging through employment records right now.

"I'd honestly rather not say, Mrs. Maxwell. I know that some level of confidentiality is required on the temp agencies end, and I'd rather not get my friend in trouble. She was immediately upset with herself for saying something and -"

"And even though she was upset, you used the information to your advantage. Ruthless, Ms. Charles." She smiled as she said it, but Zoey wasn't convinced this conversation was completely over.

"I've got a call in ten minutes. You may sit in my office to listen in, if you'd like."

"Thank you, Jemma. I really appreciate it." Zoey said with a measured amount of enthusiasm, just as the coordinator's voice came over the earpiece with the name Savannah Goetz. She filed that information away in case she needed it later.

"Of course, Katie. Why don't you head next door and grab us each a coffee before we get started?" She paused and looked at Zoey for just another moment as if there was something else she wanted to say, but instead gave a small half-smile and went to her office.

"Is anyone going to feel guilty if Jemma pushes me for a name and Savannah Goetz gets fired as a result?"

"When did you start feeling guilty about things, Zoey?"

"I didn't. I don't. I just usually know more about the people I use as covers, that's all."

The Director's next words were clipped. "You've got eight minutes remaining to get coffee before Jemma's call. But please, continue acting as though you have *my* job."

"I'm sorry, sir. That wasn't my intention. Going to get the coffee now."

Stop feeling, Zoey. Pull yourself together. The last thing you want is to get back on his bad side right now. Or his worse side, since he's still mad about me being late the other day. Why am I freaking out right now? I've got to get myself under control.

And she did. She took one deep breath and almost ran from the bank to the coffee shop. Once she got there, a massive line had formed. *Of course it has. It's almost 8:30. People are cramming in here before work. Man, I wasted a lot of time getting over here.*

Zoey tapped her foot impatiently as she waited for the line to move. Apparently, she looked stressed enough, because the couple in front of her offered their place in line. *This could work.* "Thank you, thank you so much. I'm just having the worst day already." *Cue tears.* "I lost my cat this morning and I couldn't find my cell phone, so I missed my boss's request for a coffee and now I'm running so behind. I just know I won't be able to get it to her before her big presentation this morning, and it's just so important to her and I just wanted everything to go right. . ." *Sniffles, more tears, cover your face like your ashamed, and...YES.* Almost everyone in line ahead of her motioned for her to move forward and, once she got her two coffees, she thanked them and sped away, with everyone calling well wishes after her.

"How dramatic."

"You reminded me I didn't need to be late, Director." She said the words without fully opening her mouth, in case anyone from the bank could see her.

"Remember that we will be able to hear her call. You need to observe her facial expressions and body language. Let us know if she writes anything down or reads from any specific notes."

"Got it."

CTRL + Z

"And Zoey? try not to feel *guilty* about spying on her."

ZOEY

Jemma's eyebrows raised slightly at Zoey as she rushed into the Assistant Vice President's office with moments to spare. Zoey ducked her head quietly as an apology, which allowed her to push back the nagging fear of facing the Director's wrath over a question she'd so stupidly asked. She made eye contact with Jemma once again when handing her one of the cups of coffee, which Jemma took and sipped as she dialed a number written on her notepad. Zoey quickly memorized the number and planned to give it to the team at headquarters as soon as she got another moment alone.

It was unlikely to lead them to any useful information, though. The call ended up addressing Mirror Bank's upcoming policy changes for mortgage loans. Zoey remained vigilantly watchful though just in case the team was able to pick out any codes. For her part, Jemma looked like she would rather be doing anything else other than having this call. *Probably thinking about her romantic little getaway this afternoon. It must be nice to take vacations.*

Zoey remained in Jemma's office for the two additionally scheduled calls, all directly related to bank business. After the last call ended, Jemma sent Zoey off for a break, telling her to return for a new assignment in thirty minutes. The agent took the opportunity to go for a brief walk outside, pulling out a burner phone and holding it up to her ear without actually calling anyone. She gave the Director and coordinator a rundown of Jemma's behavior during the call and supplied them with the phone numbers she had seen. The Director gave instructions for the numbers to be traced, then told Zoey to check in if anything else came up that afternoon.

Sufficiently chilled from the time outdoors, Zoey pocketed her phone and returned to the bank through the employee entrance in the back. Jemma was waiting for her and beckoned for Zoey to follow her to a room further into the depths of the bank. Just as Zoey realized someone was walking behind her, she felt a small prick just above her right shoulder, and everything faded to black.

ZOEY

When Zoey woke up, she was in a leather chair, her wrists bound to the sturdy wooden arms. She immediately noticed a complete silence in her head and panic coursed through her. Her earpiece was gone. She couldn't use the secret phrase to let anyone at the compound know she was in trouble. Sure, she had the implanted GPS device, but she suspected she was still somewhere within the bank, which meant no alarms would be triggered on her team's end. Zoey longed for the stern voice of the Director, even if he was telling her how much trouble she'd be in for getting caught.

"Hello, Zoey."

The agent stiffened slightly. Jemma knew her real name and, judging by the way she walked confidently into Zoey's view, it didn't seem she was concerned with hiding who she was. *She doesn't plan to let me live.*

Upon making eye contact, Jemma gave Zoey a small, sad smile. She didn't immediately speak; instead, she waited for her husband to enter the room, lock the door, and join her in front of the restrained woman.

"I have some things to explain to you, Zoey, but I don't know how long we have before anyone realizes we've taken your earpiece. If you will agree to simply listen to what Todd and I tell you, we'll return it to you and you'll be free to go. Do you agree to those terms?"

There's no way these two are letting me go anywhere, Zoey thought. *But maybe I can stall them long enough for the Director to realize communication has been cut...*

"What if you untie me first? Then I'll listen to whatever you have to say." She kept her voice even and calm, despite the overwhelming need to hear from the Director.

"We can't talk to you if you're attacking us, Zoey." Todd spoke up, his eyes slightly narrowed. "Jemma, I still believe this is a waste of time. We should just pull her out. Make a clean break."

Wait. What?

"You know we can't do that Todd. It has to be her choice."

"She's been there too long. She'll never believe anything we say right now. If we let her go back there, it could blow everything for us."

Zoey blinked her eyes in confusion but said nothing. The longer they argued, the more likelihood someone would figure out she was offline.

"And if we don't let her make the decision for herself, she will always search for a way to go back. That's even more dangerous for us. You know it is."

Todd looked like he wanted to continue arguing but sighed and looked at his watch instead.

"She's been offline for five minutes." Jemma nodded, then turned her attention back to Zoey.

"We'll give you cover on the time you've been offline. You'll be able to say I asked you to work on a project in a room behind the vault. The steel walls are so thick, the signal dropped. You can say that you didn't realize you were disconnected until you were well into the project.

Zoey, DNP is not what you think it is. The Board is not a typical board of directors as you believe. Trust me, I know this sounds farfetched, but the Board is actually a cover for the Shadow Dynasty. Have you heard of them?"

A Shadow Dynasty? This woman is actually insane. What does that even mean?

She didn't answer Jemma, still feeling as though she should draw this out as long as possible. When Jemma spoke again, it was with more urgency in her tone.

"I'm not sure if you're tuning me out completely or what is going on, but I need you to hear me, Zoey. The Shadow Dynasty's entire plan is to force others into their service. They have a very tight hold on the Director similar to the one he has on you. Once the Dynasty is satisfied that you're completely under his control, they'll use you to bring in a new recruit. The cycle just keeps going, and they'll destroy you when they're finished. You won't know how to live without them, but you'll never know a normal, happy life without them. We can get you out of there though. We can show you what your life could really be like. No more pushing out your feelings, no more blindly following orders. You could have friends, and even a family. You just -"

Jemma was cut off as Zoey laughed hollowly.

"I don't need a family, Jemma. Families toss you aside as soon as they are done using you. I really have no idea what you're trying to do here, especially with this ridiculous story about shadow people or whatever, but you've lost your mind if you think I'd ever turn on the Director or DNP. So, either kill me now, or let me go."

"You're not listening, Zoey. We don't want to kill you. We want to *save* you."

"She isn't going to listen to us, Jemma, and we're already ten minutes offline. We either have to extract her against her will now or let her go." Todd seemed all too keen on the idea of extracting her, and Zoey braced herself for a fight. She knew she could at least land one good kick, then try to break the arms of the chair and make a run for it if she had to. Wanting to draw their attention away from her unrestrained legs, she struggled against the binds on her arms.

"You're not extracting me to anywhere, Todd. Let me go, now." She glared at him, challenging him to walk closer to her, but Jemma placed her hand on his shoulder to stop him instead. She walked around behind Zoey and whispered softly.

"Please, just think about what we've told you. Keep your eyes open when your back at DNP. We will be here for you when you're ready." She then leaned forward and released Zoey's arms before walking across the room, unlocking and opening the door. "You'll find your earpiece is with Edna in a locked box. I think we can safely say you've completed your 'work assignments' for today. Unless you'd like to stay for a while, 'Katie'?"

The agent jumped from her chair and stormed from the room, not bothering to look at either Todd or Jemma. She didn't even speak to Edna as the elderly lady held out a soundproof box. She swiped it from her hands and ran to her car, desperately needing contact with the Director.

DIRECTOR

"Check in, check in. Hello? Is anyone there? Please tell me someone's listening. Hello?"

The Director frowned as he heard Zoey's voice fill the room's audio.

Why does she sound panicked? This isn't like her. Did the mission go sideways? I knew this was a terrible idea. I should have fought the Board more forcefully when they told me to make this assignment. What am I going to do without her?

"HELLO??"

"Zoey, you have the Director. What's wrong? What happened?"

He heard a small sigh of relief, and then quiet.

"Zoey, I'm not in the mood for games right now, what is going on out there?"

"Nothing!" She said too loudly and quickly for his comfort. "Nothing, I just.... I was just working on a project and realized my earpiece wasn't working in that part of the bank. I'm just, you know, I'm just not used to having no one respond to me. Sorry, I guess I'm just on edge or something. I think I didn't sleep well last night."

He knew she didn't sleep well last night. He also knew she had disobeyed the lights out order and stayed up entirely too late. Again. She was running on much too high of a sleep deficit; an issue he had already planned to correct with her upon her return this evening. It was Friday, so he'd have all weekend to make sure she learned her lesson. Still, he was surprised that she'd let herself get so worked up. Sure, he'd missed hearing from her in the last fifteen or twenty minutes, but he could usually make it an hour or so before losing his temper.

"We can debrief about dead zones in the bank when you return tonight. How late does Jemma plan to keep you?" He kept his voice even and cool, all the while wondering if this meant he was making progress or if she was regressing.

"She uh...um. She and Todd were planning to go away this weekend, sort of last minute. So, she told me once I finished the last project she gave me I could just leave. I'm in my car now, actually."

"Come straight to the conference room for a debriefing when you return. And no detours on the way home."

"Yes, sir."

He inclined his head a bit. She didn't say okay, or fine, or anything like that. She didn't complain. She'd given him the answer she was supposed to give him. Maybe it really was progress after all.

ZOEY

Zoey took a deep, steadying breath as she started the car and prepared to exit the parking lot. She had no logical explanation for not telling the Director immediately about her conversation with the Maxwells. She knew she could mention it in the debriefing and just play it off as though she didn't want to discuss it too close to the bank. But for some reason, she was torn on whether she would even tell him then. Honestly, the power couple had sounded like they may have done a little too much cocaine the night before. Then again, they knew Zoey's real name and knew she was an agent for DNP. And that she'd been wearing an earpiece. Clearly, her cover was blown, and it was unlikely she'd get any more information from them now. Plus, it likely wasn't safe for her to even return to the bank on Monday morning. Even processing all of that information, she couldn't shake the idea that she needed to spend more time with them.

Actually, it's best for the Director if I don't tell him. Right? I can go back in and see if they bring him or DNP up again. That way I'll know if they are plotting something against him. I can interfere before they pull the trigger on anything and, if it turns out they're crazy and had a lucky guess at my name, the Director doesn't pull me out for nothing. I mean, it had to be a lucky guess. Maybe I'd accidentally muttered it when they'd drugged me. Either way, there's no reason not to see how this plays out. Right? Right. Right...

She spent the rest of her drive back to DNP attempting to don and maintain a calm and collected attitude. She knew the last thing she needed to do after her inexplicable panic attack was to antagonize the Director. He would already be looking for signs that something was off and making him angry would just increase the scrutiny on her. She decided to be on her best behavior. *That's what he's been after all this time anyway. Maybe if I just speak as little as possible and do whatever he wants, I can keep what happened today from slipping out.* Zoey never minded the all-around work associated with being an agent, but it had never felt right to her to just comply with all things at all times.

After parking her car in the underground lot, she put on her best blank face and walked quietly through the DNP compound until she reached the conference room. She was the first to arrive, so she sat in the chair to the left of the Director's typical chair, knowing that's where he preferred her during briefings. Zoey sat forward slightly, her back straight, and crossed her hand on the table. She didn't move again until the Director came into the room. As he walked through the doorframe she stood, waiting for him, Trevor, and the field coordinator to enter. The Director sat in the chair she knew he would, and the others followed suit. He looked up at Zoey as if he were considering something, then spoke.

"You may sit, Zoey."

And so she did, quickly and quietly, back into the position she'd been in while waiting for his arrival. The rest of the team looked bewildered, looking at Zoey, then each other, then to the Director, who leaned back in his chair a bit, turning it to face the young woman.

"You said you lost comms today?"

"Yes, sir." She spoke quietly, but with the conviction she knew he expected. As the two made eye contact, she could tell he was a bit thrown off, and she immediately began to wonder if this had been the right call. It was too late to back down now though. The others had already seen the behavior and she had no doubt that the retribution from the Director if she did an about-face right now would not be worth it. She maintained eye contact and waited until he spoke again.

"Explain that to me. No one on our end picked up any disturbance. When did you realize you'd lost contact, and what were you doing? How long did you wait before you called a check-in?" His calm demeanor was so unnerving to her that she had to wonder if he felt the same way about her current behavior. *Oh well.*

"Yes, sir. Jemma asked me to work through some old hard copy documents the bank had in a storage room slightly behind the vault. She wanted me to place anything before ten years ago into boxes for shredding. I was working through them, reviewing all of them as quickly as I could to see if any information stood out. I muttered something under my breath, and I was just surprised that no one responded to it. So, I said some things a little louder to test the system. I wasn't sure if you could hear me or not, but I definitely couldn't hear you. Jemma had told me I could leave as soon as I finished the project, so I just pushed through and wrapped up. There was probably only a ten-minute gap between when I noticed and when I got to my car."

Why am I doing this?

"You were reviewing documents that Jemma Maxwell intended to shred."

"Yes, sir."

"And why exactly did you not put on your glasses so you could scan all of those documents for the team here to review, so that we could see if there was anything important in them?"

Crap.

"I... I honestly didn't think about it."

"You didn't think about it?" She almost preferred the edge to his voice over the earlier calm, but the calm is really what she needed today.

"I'm sorry, sir."

"It's interesting to me that you're acting the way you are right now, Zoey."

"Sir?" *This is it. This is where he tells me he knows what happened or he knows I'm lying, or something awful happens or-*

"You must know that I'm aware of your refusal to follow your lights out policies this week."

Oh, thank God.

Before she could respond, he continued.

"I've been telling you for years that these rules were in place for *your* benefit, Zoey. Yet you always seem to fight me on them. And now, you've gone four nights without sufficient sleep, and you're making mistakes. Rookie mistakes. You should have had those glasses on before you even got to the file room. But here we are, without additional information we could have used without even working for it. That's why you're so docile right now. You know you screwed up!"

"Yes, sir." Zoey spoke almost inaudibly, trying to hold in a deep sigh of relief. This was the kind of trouble she could handle, and she knew he'd be pleased when she accepted her punishment for breaking the childish and unnecessary curfew.

"Then if nothing else happened today, head to containment immediately. I'll come see you when I decide it's worth my time to talk to you. You're dismissed."

"Yes, sir." She spoke once more, stood from her chair and exited the room. She acknowledged no one on her way to containment and, once inside, found herself actually relieved to have a moment alone to regroup.

ZOEY

Sitting back in containment once again, Zoey replayed the conversation with Jemma and Todd in her mind over and over until her mind was numb. Their story was so farfetched, so out of the blue that it couldn't possibly be real. Especially the part about a Shadow Dynasty. Even if there was some absurd possibility that such a thing existed, she didn't even know where to begin digging. She surely couldn't walk up to the Director and ask him point-blank. He'd have her locked up in medical before she could claim it was a joke.

She thought back to the day they'd left Camp together, when she'd had a realization that she was nothing more than a prisoner at DNP. A tool to be used for missions, with no autonomy and no freedom. Those thoughts hadn't crossed her mind really since then, with everything going much smoother at headquarters.

Great, now this ridiculous story has me doubting things. Even if I'm just here to do a job, it's not at the behest of some ominous beings determined to destroy the lives of random, everyday people.

She rested her arms against her legs and placed her hands over her face, trying desperately to dismiss the entire situation.

"What's going on?"

The Director's voice completely startled Zoey. She hadn't even heard the door open, which wasn't a good sign. She silently prayed she wouldn't get in trouble for not being more aware of her surroundings.

"Nothing, I just...I was just thinking about how I missed a great opportunity for intel and honestly, I'm feeling pretty stupid about it."

She wasn't entirely sure the answer satisfied him as she watched him lean against the wall opposite her, so she stood up before speaking again.

"I never make mistakes like that, and I'm frustrated that I did."

He considered the response, then changed the subject.

"Have you learned anything more about the receptionist? Edna?"

"She..." Zoey knew she needed to give him something to redeem herself, but what? "I think she knows a lot more about what Jemma and Todd are up to than we realized. It's almost like she is set up to hear what's going on in their offices, because she knows when I'm heading her way if that makes sense."

That was much better than telling him that Edna clearly knew she was an agent of some type and had held her earpiece hostage earlier in the day.

"Have you noticed her wearing anything that could be a device?"

"Maybe her earrings? She changes them out though…She does wear the same pearl necklace every day, but it looks like an antique."

"Could you get behind her to look at the clasp?"

"I'm sure I can, I'll have to time it right. Like I said, she always looks like she's expecting me when I go by her desk."

"I'll get Trevor to put together something you can use to do an actual scan on her without her noticing." A brief awkward silence followed, and Zoey noticed the Director was now actively avoiding eye contact as he spoke again.

"Jemma and Todd. Have either of them said or done anything around you that feels…off?"

Yeah, they told me you basically kidnapped me to turn me into a disciple of an otherworldly set of monsters who want me to recruit new souls for them.

"Honestly, they just seem like they have a lot of secrets. I can almost never catch them together, and Todd rarely even acts like he notices me. I have noticed that…" She stopped herself, not sure how to word the idea that they had fundamentally differing views on how to approach certain situations without giving an actual example.

"What?"

"What?"

"Zoey, you said you noticed that…what?"

He was back to making eye contact now, and he looked very much annoyed.

"Oh, sorry, I guess I lost my train of thought."

"There's literally nothing in this room to distract you Zoey, so I need you to put in a little bit of effort here."

"I just noticed that maybe...maybe they don't necessarily agree on as many things as most people think? Sometimes I can feel kind of a tension between them. Like they aren't really getting along or something."

Great, now he's going to have me looking into nonexistent marital problems.

"Do you remember what I told you by the fountain a few days ago?"

"It's a dangerous mission. Stay focused, remember everything. We have to be successful."

"It seems like you're struggling with the staying focused part."

He genuinely seemed concerned about her now, and that made her feel even worse about lying to him. *Withholding, not lying. Definitely not lying.*

"I swear I'm staying focused. If I just had more information on what we're looking for, that would help. I can spy on their work product all day but mostly they seem like a normal couple who just happen to work together."

"I'm not giving you more details because I want to know *everything*. Even if you think it's completely irrelevant or completely normal. I want to know every single thing you see and hear when you're there. I want to know how Jemma likes to part her hair and how Todd speaks to other employees. I want to know how much involvement Edna has with them and if she has that same level with other employees. I want to know what time they take bathroom breaks or smoke breaks or meal breaks. Every single thing you can notice, I want you to share with me."

"This isn't about the documents we translated, is it?"

He sighed.

"You're still not listening. It doesn't matter what it's about right now. It's about you getting every bit of intel you can as quickly as we can. We can't assess any other issues that we may or may not be tracking unless you do that first."

"Yes, sir." She still didn't fully understand what he was going on about, but his level of agitation was growing, and she wanted to diffuse the situation before it ended even more poorly for her than time in containment.

"Let's go."

Her eyebrows rose.

"Go where?" She immediately regretted asking.

"Well, I thought you *might* want to join the rest of us in the dining hall for dinner but if you'd prefer to spend the rest of the weekend here…" he gestured to the room.

"Dinner sounds great actually, thank you." The words flew from her mouth. If she was being given a get out of jail card, she was going to take it, even if she didn't understand the reason for it. Neither one of them spoke again until they had reached the doors to the dining hall.

CTRL + Z

"You can have whatever you'd like tonight." Then he opened the door and walked toward some of the coordinators who were gathered at a table to the left, greeting them as if they were a group of friends meeting up after a day of work. Zoey went through the line, picking out a deliciously gigantic plate of loaded nachos, and went to sit with some other agents across the room, enjoying herself for the first time in quite a while.

ZOEY

Zoey and the other agents she sat with ended up hanging out in the dining hall late that evening, trading stories and playing various card and board games. She had noticed the Director looking at her before he left with some of the others, but he didn't indicate that she should leave, so she allowed herself to relax and enjoy the time. By 10:30, the cleaning staff was shooing them out, lecturing them for staying so late. They all apologized, though not one of them looked the slightest bit remorseful for the impromptu party. They meandered slowly back toward the cabins when one agent suggested they all go outside for a bit instead.

Can I do this? Can I really go up there without permission? Should I tell them I'm tired? If he didn't want me following them up, then he definitely would have told me to leave earlier. And it's not like I'm going to actually go anywhere, just be out in the fresh air. And he'll be able to see where I am. This is fine. Totally.

And so she convinced herself to go outside with the others, where they all sat around the fountain telling jokes and acting as carefree as she imagined people with normal jobs were. At one point, she slipped off the fountain edge causing her and the others to laugh loudly as she hit the water. When she stood, she thought for the briefest moment that she could see the Director looking out at them through his window. But after another agent helped her step out of the fountain, she looked back, and no one was there. She remained outside, soaking wet, until everyone was finally ready to call it a night.

Saturday morning, Zoey woke up feeling well-rested. She hadn't realized how badly she'd needed some downtime. It made sense though; she had worked four back-to-back missions before her time in containment and at Camp. Then, she'd pretty much jumped right back into another mission. While she was glad to have things mostly back to normal, she was frustrated by the lack of real information on the Maxwells, and she had definitely been feeling some stress after their "conversation." Especially so after lying to the Director about it. Having time to take her mind off all those things for an evening and then getting to sleep well made Zoey feel like a whole new person. Up until the AI voice came through the speakers in her room, that is.

"Hello, Agent Z. The Director requests your presence in his office immediately."

Great. Here comes a lecture on staying up too late or going outside without permission.

Zoey threw her covers off her and stretched, noticing a scrape on her knee from falling into the fountain. She smiled to herself as she got out of the bed and went to the bathroom to brush her teeth and attempt to fix her unmanageable hair. Eventually she gave up and tied it back in a ponytail, then dressed in her favorite dark-wash jeans with a pair of black sneakers and a purple top, with a black unzipped hoodie. It *was* Saturday, after all.

When she arrived at the Director's office, his door was closed. She knocked, but there was no answer, so she leaned back against the wall next to the door and waited. She could tell there was someone in there with him, but their voices were too low to make out who it was or what they were saying. *Probably for the best. He'd be furious if he thought I was eavesdropping.*

DIRECTOR

"You haven't been on any assignments lately because you haven't proven that you can do your job without it turning into abject disaster."

The Director spat the words out at the agent across from him. He'd been planning to speak to Zoey when Michael asked for a moment to speak with him, and the Director was regretting allowing him. Michael had been an agent for about five years and was Zoey's age, but he was hotheaded in a way that Zoey wasn't. They'd had to send cleanup crews after his last three consecutive assignments, so the Director had put him at a desk and assigned him to assisting the translations department.

"I know a few of them got a little out of hand, but they were all successful. If I could just have another chance to prove myself to you-"

"This isn't kindergarten, Michael. We don't give out participation trophies. I don't consider wasting time and resources cleaning up a mess that *you* made to be successful."

"But, Sir, I just want-"

"ENOUGH. You will get back in the field if and when I decide to allow it. Until then, prove that you can follow directions by doing the job I've given you, or we will have to reevaluate whether you really belong at DNP."

He watched as Michael blanched at his words before stuttering out a "yes, sir."

"Get out of my office and tell Zoey I'll be with her in a moment."

Michael rushed out of the room, and the Director sank into his chair, sighing. He hadn't wanted to be in a bad mood for this conversation. Not after he saw how happy Zoey looked last night, as though she could be perfectly content here at DNP forever. With him. He didn't want his agitation with Michael to seep into the conversation he'd wanted to have with her.

"Come in, Zoey."

The first thing he noticed when she walked in was how *normal* she looked, like a typical young woman going out to run errands on the weekend. He motioned for her to sit in one of the guest chairs across from his desk and she did, sitting with her right leg folded under her and her left foot on the ground. *She's comfortable here with me today.*

"You were out late last night."

"Oh," her face fell immediately, "I'm sorry, I know I've been staying up late and I shouldn't-"

He waved a hand at her to dismiss the apology.

"I'm actually not angry, Zoey, I was simply making an observation."

As she nodded her head, he quickly tried to get her back to her carefree mood.

"Perhaps you don't spend enough time with the other agents. Even before all that's happened recently, you mostly kept to yourself. I think the interaction is good for you."

Her soft smile was exactly what he needed to bring him back from the foul mood he'd acquired just a few moments ago.

"I do need to talk to you about your current assignment briefly, but I wanted you to know I think you should join the others in the dining hall for your meals today."

"Yes, sir." She was almost grinning, and he warmed inside. *The Board will be so happy with my work. They will love that she is willing to stay here forever, and I will finally be rewarded for my hard work.*

"Regarding the Maxwells, I do realize I haven't given you enough information. This is confidential, Zoey, not even the rest of the field team knows what I'm about to tell you. We have reason to believe that they have created a company to rival DNP, and that they plan to start poaching our agents. We don't know how much information they might have, if they have any at all. That is why we *must* know everything we can about them. We need you to get closer."

She looked away from him, as if he she was considering his explanation. *I hate when she looks away from me.*

"That makes sense," she finally said, her words coming out slowly. "Given...whatever mission they were planning through those documents we translated. I'll watch as closely as I can."

"Thank you, and please, remember to watch your back. If they really are going after our agents and they find out who you are…"

She made eye contact once again.

"I promise I'll be safe."

"Good. Why don't you go get breakfast? Try to enjoy the rest of your weekend and we will all reconvene Sunday evening to make any additional plans we need to for the week." Then he watched as she stood up, hesitating as if she were going to say something else, and then she left, closing the door behind her. *I guess now's a good time to call an update into the Board.*

ZOEY

I can make this work. I just need to find a way to get Jemma and Todd to talk to me again without my earpiece in and then I can tell the Director they confronted me. That way he doesn't know I never told him about what happened Friday. This is going to be okay.

She was actually relieved that the Director provided the additional information. Now it all made sense to her. They were trying to get into her head, threatening to "extract" her and coming up with the ridiculous story they told her, but they really just wanted to recruit her to their own agency. That made sense to Zoey. She could handle that type of threat.

She allowed various scenarios for Monday to play through her mind as she made her way to the dining hall for breakfast, and found she wasn't very hungry after the massive plate of nachos she'd had the night before. She grabbed an apple and a water and joined the same group but said her goodbyes quickly so she could return to her cabin and make plans.

ZOEY

Adrenaline pumped through Zoey early Monday morning as she drove toward the bank. She was ready to get things rolling now that she knew what the Maxwells were really trying to do, and she desperately wanted to be able to hand over as much information as she could get to the Director. Once she was parked and inside, she grabbed a sheet of paper and wrote a small note on it- "Ask me to do a project in the room from last time so Edna can hold my earpiece and we can talk for a few minutes." She really wanted Jemma and Todd to think she'd been stewing all weekend, trying to dig up dirt on the Director for them, but she had to be careful. Crafting her own plan meant the Director and rest of the team would always be a step behind Zoey as things unfolded. This could pose a serious problem if 1) the Director found out she was keeping him slightly in the dark and 2) if the Maxwells caught on and were able to take some sort of action against Zoey before she could alert anyone at headquarters. *I guess the second possibility would probably be the worst one, though, since if that happened the Director would definitely find out.*

She slipped the note into the back pocket of her slacks and started milling around the bank, trying to look busy. As she rounded a corner to the front atrium, she heard Edna speaking to another bank employee. Zoey tugged slightly at the ring Trevor had made that the Director had given her that morning, making sure it was ready to scan as she approached the front desk. Edna remained facing the other employee, so Zoey waved her hand in an almost exaggerated gesture as she said hello, allowing the ring to scan the back of Edna's necklace. She didn't see anything particularly unusual about the clasp, but she knew from firsthand experience how easily one could hide technology.
Edna turned toward her, smiling softly.

"Hi, Katie. I hope you had a good weekend?"
Oh, this woman knows everything they are up to. I can tell.

"I did, Edna! Look, my fiancé proposed!" She waved her hand up and down in front of her, allowing it to scan across Edna once more.

"Oh my! I didn't know you were seeing anyone, dear! How lovely!" Edna looked confused, but beamed at Zoey, nonetheless.

"Thank you, I'm so excited. I'll have to ask Trevor to stop by and meet you one day!"

In her earpiece she heard Trevor respond.

"I didn't realize we were in a relationship either, Zoey. You should have bought me chocolates or something."

"Anyway, Edna, I better get back to work, I just wanted to share my news with you!"

Zoey half skipped away trying to look as girlishly excited as possible, an act which she dropped once around the corner where she heard the Director's voice.

"Great job Zoey. It looks like one of the pearls in the front of her necklace houses a microphone and her glasses have an earpiece in the left side. Trevor will start working on a way to tap into those feeds." *Hopefully he isn't able to do it before I have my meeting.*

As she turned down the next hallway, she saw Jemma and Todd having a hushed conversation just outside of Jemma's office. *Perfect timing!* Zoey fished the small note out of her pocket, slipping it into Jemma's hands as they greeted each other. After Jemma finished reading the note, she handed it to Todd to read, who nodded and headed toward the older rooms.

"Katie, why don't you step into my office for just a moment so I can get my thoughts around your next project."

"Of course, Jemma. How was your weekend getaway?" Zoey followed Jemma into her office and waited patiently while the woman took off her coat and put away her purse, straightening some things on her desk and telling Zoey how great a time she'd had. Once she seemed settled, she used her speakerphone to call Edna.

"Hi, Edna. I have another project in the back with Katie today. Could you stop by my office to get some things to take to the loan processing department before I take her back to get started?"

"Why of course! And make sure she shows you that *beautiful* engagement ring if she hasn't already!"

Jemma raised her eyebrows and looked up at Zoey, who flashed a huge grin as she lifted up her left hand.

"I didn't realize you were in a serious relationship, Katie."

Zoey giggled softly. "I *do* have a life outside of work, Jemma."

"I'm glad to hear that." And she actually did look like she was happy that Zoey had time for dating. They waited just a moment for Edna to arrive and Jemma handed her a stack of papers before indicating that they were going to discuss the next project. The Director spoke over Zoey's earpiece.

"Don't panic if you lose us again. Just do what you need to do and report back. If you're dealing with any documents or anything potentially valuable, put your glasses on once Jemma has left and we'll figure it out."

"I'm ready to get started!" She said aloud to Jemma, knowing the Director would understand she was acknowledging her comment. Edna quietly followed them to the room where Zoey had previously been held captive and pulled the small box from before out of a pocket. Zoey smiled and slipped her earpiece into it and watched as Edna turned back toward the lobby. She straightened her shoulders, took a deep breath, and went inside to see Jemma and Todd whispering once again. Zoey closed the door behind her and began implementation of her off-the-books plan.

ZOEY

"So, who is the lucky guy?" Jemma asked, her attention on Zoey once more.

"I don't think we have time to discuss my romantic life, Jemma. And you certainly know that's not why I wanted this meeting."

"Why *did* you want this meeting? You made it pretty clear you had no interest in what we had to say on Friday," Todd interjected. He looked annoyed and rolled his eyes as Jemma waved him off before trying to get things back on track.

"I am surprised, Zoey, that you've requested this meeting so quickly. Were you able to find anything out?"

"First of all, I think it's best for all of us if you continue calling me Katie even when we are back here. Second, I want you to tell me how you got any information on the Director to begin with, and why you even care."

"Very well, *Katie*. As I said before, we are working against the Shadow Dynasty. That's how we knew who the Director was. We had no idea who they'd assigned to him, and then you happened to fall right into our laps. So maybe you can tell me-how you came by your assignment?"

"I have no reason to share any information with you yet. As far as I know, you're both lunatics raving about nightmares you had while high or something. I don't want to hear about some stupid dynasty. I just want to know what your endgame is here."

"Jemma, seriously. Let's just pull her out. She's not in contact with them. By the time they realize she's missing, they won't have any way of finding her."

"If you think you can physically overpower me to take me anywhere Todd, you're very mistaken, but I'd be happy to let you try." Zoey took a defensive position, still ready to strike the moment Todd took one wrong step.

"We won't be trying to force you to go anywhere right now, Katie." Jemma positioned herself between the two, looking at Todd as if to command him to back down.

"I can't explain our interest in the Director without talking to you about the Shadow Dynasty. They are too interconnected. I can tell you that you're not safe, and that your life is not your own. Whatever relationship you think you might have with your fiancé; I guarantee you it is ultimately engineered by the Director. Your happiness is not important to him or the Dynasty. They will allow you to maintain the illusion of it for as long as it serves their purpose, and then they will rip it away from you. They want you in their service, under their control, no matter the cost to you.

Todd and I had a run-in with the Shadow Dynasty before; they tried to bring us into their service. That's how we met, actually. We don't want any part of what they are attempting to accomplish, though, and would rather fight back. That's why we created NLS, a company similar to your DNP. We are actively working to rescue those under the Dynasty's control. Not just at DNP, either. Honestly, for all we know, you're the only person there besides the Director who the Dynasty has gotten. But there are people all over the world in different jobs, different walks of life, who are falling to the Dynasty, and that number is growing daily. Do you know the real stories of the people you are targeting on missions? They are the ones who got away from the Dynasty. You're being sent to eliminate them. If they won't bow to the Dynasty, the Dynasty has no use for them. We want you to join us and help us stop them from ruining so many lives. You all deserve the opportunity to live your lives for yourself, make your own decisions. When was the last time you got to do that?

Think about it. Are you allowed to come and go from your base as you please? When you leave here in the evenings, if you're really meeting a fiancé, do you have to get permission? Are you monitored constantly? Most people aren't forced to live that way. You could have so many more choices and opportunities."

I can't even eat what or when I want. Zoey's head was spinning, but she had to stay focused. The Director told her they'd do this-they'd try to turn her to their side. But she wouldn't be fooled so easily.

"And how do I know you don't immediately place your agents under the same conditions? If you're really trying to rival DNP, you'll have to have some sort of authority or control over your agents."

"Our agents are free to stop working with us at any time. When we bring in those who have been controlled by the Dynasty for a long time, people like you, we don't immediately put them in the field. We help them adjust to a new, healthy, happy life. Then they get to choose for themselves if they want to join our cause."

"Then why does Wild West over here keep talking about forcing me out of DNP?"

"Ultimately, we won't be able to remain on friendly terms if you stay with DNP. We want you to leave and we want your help because we know how good you are at what you do. Eventually, though, we will have to take action. If you choose DNP, if you choose the Director and the Dynasty, you'll be working directly against us. Todd thinks it would be safer for us and for you if we pulled you out of DNP now. Honestly, he's not entirely wrong about that, but it's clear you have a job to do for DNP here right now. We can keep our eyes on you just as you keep your eyes on us, and that gives you time to make a decision on your own. We *will* be keeping an eye on you, though, and if you become too big of a risk for us, we may have to choose to follow Todd's path." She fidgeted with a bead on her bracelet.

"And what if I leave here today and go share every bit of this with the Director?"

"You could do that, but I don't think you will. You're a smart girl. I can't imagine you would rush into a decision on this without taking the time to gather some more information."

A knock at the door interrupted the conversation and Edna entered, holding out Zoey's earpiece. She took it and placed it back in her ear just before Jemma spoke again.

"Honestly though this project may not be quite ready. Why don't you do some filing and then join me for lunch at noon? We can discuss allowing you to shadow some of the other bank officers to learn what they do."

A voice in Zoey's ear said, "No lunch. I'll send dinner to your room when you return for the evening."

"Thank you, Jemma, but I actually already have lunch plans today. I'll be ready to observe anyone you'd like when you get back though."

Jemma's face fell at Zoey's answer, as if she knew that the Director had intervened, but she didn't acknowledge it. Rather, she simply nodded and left the room, Todd following silently behind her. Zoey let out a long breath before heading to the filing room, finding there was nothing there to file. Once she realized she actually had a window of free time, she went to her car to pretend to talk on the phone.

DIRECTOR

"Okay, so…there's a lot going on here. Jemma and Todd are apparently really trying to get an agency up and running that is similar to DNP. They called it NLS, so maybe we can look into any business registration records they may have filed. They don't seem to have any idea that I'm not Katie Charles, but they definitely tried to recruit me. Jemma said they were looking for highly motivated individuals to be part of their team. The way she described it, I think NLS is going to be a nefarious version of DNP. While we are out here working governmental contracts and things, I think they will actually be trying to undermine DNP. It's going to take a little time to dig into it more, but this is definitely an issue. And one other thing, I think Jemma has some sort of button or something on her bracelet that allows her to tell Edna she's needed. She fidgeted with it for just a moment before Edna showed up to the door. That also leads me to believe that Edna is part of whatever NLS is doing."

The Director drummed his fingers on the conference table as Zoey filled him and the rest of the team in on the conversation she'd had with Jemma.

"Why don't we let them recruit Zoey? Have her play along with it for a while, so we gather intel?" The field captain spoke up, still looking at his copious notes.

"No." *How can I handle this without Zoey knowing I slipped a bug on her when I personally delivered her breakfast this morning?* "No, that's too dangerous until we know a little more. I don't want them finding out who Zoey is while she's out of our reach."

That sounded good. He was furious, though, to find out that she'd lied to him before when her comms went down, and that she hadn't told him she planned to talk to them again. Of course, he'd known something was off with her story about Friday. She'd been far too panicked by losing a connection and she was much more compliant than he'd anticipated. It's why he slid the listening device into the base of the ring just before walking into Zoey's room. He was the only one at DNP who'd heard the entire conversation that morning, and he couldn't fathom how easily the Maxwells found it to talk about the Shadow Dynasty. He only referred to them as the Board and had never considered discussing their business openly. He was thankful that, at least for now, Zoey didn't believe a word they'd said about the Dynasty. But they'd still done enough potential damage. He had no idea how he was going to address the situation with Zoey, either. If he punished her for lying, it might push her closer to them. If he didn't act at all, she may think she could continue her errant behavior in the future. He was in a very precarious situation, and he needed to figure it out before his next report to the Board.

"Zoey, why don't you pretend you're feeling under the weather and tell them you need to take the rest of the day off? Surely they won't push the issue, given the amount of information they dumped on you." There was a brief pause before she responded.

"Yes, sir."

ZOEY

He doesn't know. There's no way he knows. He's just worried about me being here until we can come up with a game plan for dealing with NLS. There's no reason to panic here.

She was panicking though because it was out of character for the Director to pull her out in the middle of the day. Regardless, she'd been given an order and wasn't keen on defying it just yet, especially since she'd only been given a half of an orange so far. She went straight to Jemma's office where she found Jemma and Edna reviewing actual bank business-related documents.

"Hey Jemma? I'm actually...not feeling so great right now. Do you think I could take off the rest of the day and start observing tomorrow?"

Jemma scribbled furiously on a notepad while Edna spoke.

"Oh honey, you do look like you aren't feeling well. Would you like me to grab you a cup of tea?"

"No thank you, Edna. That's very sweet of you though," Zoey said as she accepted the note from Jemma. It read, "Are you safe? Do you need our help? Should we pull you out?"

"I really just feel like I need to lie down for a bit," she said, while still giving Jemma thumbs up and mouthing that she was fine. Jemma eyed her suspiciously before finally telling her to get some rest and that she hoped she felt better quickly.

Zoey's thoughts raced as she drove back to headquarters. She considered that the Director wouldn't have made a big deal out of knowing more than he let on while she was out of his reach but, then again, he had the GPS tracker, and she didn't know how far the range on the interrogation simulation chip was just yet.

I should figure that out. Wait, no. It doesn't matter. I'm not going anywhere. I'm not interested in NLS. Maybe he thinks I am *interested. Maybe that's why he's acting strange. It probably wouldn't hurt to know the range, just for my own safety. He didn't let me have lunch, though. But then he wanted me to get back quickly, so that probably means he was just worried about getting me out of a potentially dangerous situation quickly.*

By the time she was almost back to headquarters she had mostly talked herself down. She was paranoid because she was doing things in a way not really allowed, but that didn't mean anyone had caught on yet. She just needed to meet with the team and act as natural as possible, giving them any additional information she could without revealing too much.

When she was walking down the hallway to the conference room, she ran into Trevor, also on his way.

"So, when's the big wedding date for us?" He grinned as he playfully shoved her shoulder.

"You know, I think I'm going to need a much, much bigger ring than this if you really want to lock me down."

"Are you sure? Because we could spend that money on a house or something more important than jewelry."

"What's more important to a girl than jewelry?"

"To a regular girl, or to a girl who loves kicking people in the face?"

"I'm sure regular girls like to kick people in the face, Trevor."

"Maybe, but they don't do it with such finesse."

She laughed, enjoying his company as they arrived at the conference room, where the Director and field coordinator were already waiting. She tried to rein in her smile when she saw the Director's face and noted that he was in an all-business mode. She took her usual seat beside him and waited quietly for him to begin the meeting.

"We were just trying to decide if we should keep you undercover, Zoey." The Director said, with concern in his eyes. He was watching her intently, she noticed, and she did her best to stay focused on his words rather than the million thoughts racing through her mind.

"Because you don't think it's safe for me to stay?"

He nodded. "If they keep pulling you further back into the bank to speak with you, we won't be able to hear if you're in trouble."

Trevor sat forward and interjected, "I can probably find a different device that will let us hear in there, even if Zoey can't hear us in response. We could hide it in a piece of jewelry or something. The ring, maybe?"

Zoey watched as the Director whipped his head toward Trevor. He looked enraged, which Trevor clearly noticed too.

"I'm sorry, sir, I was just trying to brainstorm options. Of course, if it's safer to just pull the mission, I absolutely get that…"

"I think the ring is too obvious a place for it," the Director finally responded, his demeanor calmed. "She just started wearing it. I would suspect it, too."

Zoey nodded. She would suspect it, too, and tried to think of other potential places to hide a listening device, unsure of whether she should actually voice those thoughts. She didn't have a chance though, as the Director spoke again.

"Trevor, you gave me a prototype of a small adhesive device, which I sent to the Board for approval. While we may be jumping the gun a bit, why don't you get a set for Zoey to stick inside the top of her shirts and dresses, and code them to one of the relay speakers you created for them. If those don't have the range we need to ensure Zoey's safety, then we'll pull her."

Trevor looked thrilled at the chance to try one of his newest pieces of work and told Zoey he'd have them delivered to her cabin that evening once he had them set up and ready to go.

"So just to be clear, I *am* going back tomorrow?" She finally asked, slightly blindsided by the Director's quick turnaround on the issue.

"Do you have a problem with that? Is there any reason you might not feel safe? Anything we don't know or aren't prepared for at this time?"

There's so much you don't know and it's not safe. Oh, also this is going to completely ruin my plans for trying to keep you from finding out I didn't disclose the first meeting I had with them.

"No, sir, I'm not concerned about my safety. And you have all the same information I do."

"Fine. Go to your cabin, then. We'll touch base again later tonight."

Zoey had really wanted to go down to the wardrobe unit to see if they had any new outfits she could snag for her days at the bank. Specifically, she wanted to make sure she could find some things that would allow her to move freely and potentially hide weapons. She had been extremely well-behaved lately, all things considered, so she decided to try her luck.

"Actually, sir, I was hoping I might be able to go see Sylvie and find out if she's gotten anything new in that I could use this week?"

If looks could kill, she would have been dead on the spot.

"Did I ask you if you *wanted* to go to your cabin, Zoey?"

Well, crap.

"No, sir."

"Did I give you any indication that you had any other options?"

"No, sir."

"Why don't you join me in my office for a more in-depth discussion of this issue?"

No, sir, I'll be in my cabin. No need to have a chat. I got the message loud and clear.

"Yes, sir." She forced the words out, immensely regretting her moment of bravery. *Or stupidity.*

The Director marched out of the room and Zoey followed, casting a quick glance to Trevor, who looked at her apologetically. He couldn't help in this situation, no one could. All she could do was be as remorseful as possible and attempt to come out of the meeting mostly unscathed.

DIRECTOR

Yet again, he found himself sitting opposite Zoey, furious with her for defying him. *This is completely unacceptable. Has she so quickly forgotten how easily I can make her life miserable? At least she's given me a reason to lash out at her other than lying to me. I'll be addressing that later, once I have a better grasp on exactly what happened.*

"Why do you keep doing this?" He asked, watching her closely for any signs that she might come clean on her own if he pushed her just far enough.

"I wasn't trying-"

"I didn't ask you what you were *trying* to do. You're never *trying* to be disrespectful, or disobey orders, or break rules. Yet somehow you keep managing to do it over and over again. I really thought we had been able to work through all of that when we left Camp last time, but here we are having another conversation about your behavior. Maybe you need to be reminded again of your place here."

He had been hiding the remote control for the interrogation chip in his palm and quickly pressed the button on it to catch her off guard. He watched as she fell forward out of her chair and cried out in pain, then turned the device back off before she started screaming. *Probably best if no one knows I'm still using this.*

The Director sat still, watching her pant as she tried to catch her breath.

"Get back up, Zoey," he commanded. To her credit, she pushed herself up from the floor immediately and stood next to the chair where she'd been sitting. He realized she was waiting for his permission to sit. *Good girl.*

"Want to lodge a complaint?"

"No, sir." Her voice was shaky and quiet.

"Louder, please."

"No, sir." She said once more, with more volume and equally more shakiness. She was definitely afraid he was going to press that tiny button again. And he *was* going to, just not quite yet.

"Are you looking for a way out of here, Zoey? Are you enticed by the offer you received today?"

She looked genuinely surprised at his question, as if the idea had never occurred to her.

"No, sir. I would never go to a rival company."

That didn't fully answer the question. Was she thinking about leaving DNP? Leaving me? I can't allow that. That was when he made the decision to just call her out. Who would she complain to when she finds out he'd spied on her? *What power did she have? Even if she was angry, it was her own fault. She lied to me first.* He would tell Trevor not to worry about the extra listening devices.

"But you've thought about it, haven't you?"

"No, sir, I haven't."

"Sure you have. What other reason could there possibly be for you *lying* to me?" The Director was speaking through gritted teeth, and Zoey flinched. He remained focused on her, knowing she was trying to weigh the possible options in her mind. He wouldn't let her off the hook easily, though.

"What's the matter, Zoey? Perhaps you thought I wouldn't find out you met with the Maxwells in secret on Friday? I hope the price for your silence was worth it to you."

He pressed the button again, and stood as she collapsed once more, writhing in agony. He allowed the pain to go on a little longer this time before stopping it. When she looked up at him with tears streaming down her face, he was reminded of the child he'd found so many years ago, which made her betrayal even more unacceptable.

"I didn't..." she gasped for air, unable to stand. "I didn't..." Though he knew she was trying to get more words out, he yelled at her.

"You *did*! Stop LYING to me!" The Director forced the pain through her again, almost relishing her pleading for it to stop.

ZOEY

He's going to kill me. When he's done playing with me like I'm nothing, he's going to kill me. I should have never lied to him. It was so stupid. I could have endangered everyone here. This hurts. Too much. I can't breathe. I can't-

"Please, please stop. Please," she cried as she begged for mercy, and he finally granted it.

"Stand up." His anger was palpable as he stood over her, glaring down as if he were angry at her weakness. Several attempts at standing were unsuccessful, and she had to use the chair to pull herself up. *I don't know how long I can stand without assistance.*

"Did you meet with Jemma and Todd Maxwell on Friday?" The Director turned his back toward her as he walked back around his desk.

"It…it wasn't a meeting…" she barely got the words out. He whipped around to face her, clearly ready to resume torturing her, and she spoke as quickly and loudly as she could in hopes it would stop him.

"They drugged me and tied me up and they took my earpiece, I swear I didn't go there to meet with them." Having used all of her energy just to speak, she fell back to the floor. Zoey kept trying to make herself stop crying; she knew how much the Director hated it. But she was overwhelmed-not only with the pain, but with the malice dripping off him.

"I don't want to have to tell you to stand up again." His words were quiet and deadly. The agent brushed her hair back behind her ears and forced herself to her feet; forced herself to meet his gaze.

"Yes, sir," she breathed.

"You were *drugged*?" Something in him seemed to shift, almost looking like concern.

"Yes, sir...I'm, I'm sorry. I just...I was worried you'd be mad that they snuck up on me, so I didn't say anything. And then I was going to try to fix it today. I should have said something. I'm sorry." She was out of breath still, feeling more lightheaded with every moment that passed.

"Sit down."

She breathed a small sigh of relief as she slowly lowered herself back into the chair, waiting as the Director returned to his own. *Wait. How did he know about the meeting? How could he have?*

"Director, may I...may I ask a question?" *I've lost my mind.*

He sat the remote down on his desk, just in front of where his hand was now resting. *At least he doesn't intend to use it again immediately. I'll be able to see it coming next time.* He sighed in annoyance.

"What is your question, Zoey?"

"I just wondered how you found out about Friday?"

"Why don't we get through all the information you need to share with me and then maybe we can talk about that."

"Yes, sir."

"I want to know every single thing that happened Friday, from the time you left here that morning until you returned. Do not leave out a single detail."

Because she feared his anger and retribution, and because it no longer made sense to keep it from him, she told him everything. Zoey had to continue pausing to catch her breath as her body was still trying to restabilize after the vicious attack on her nervous system. When she finished recounting the entire day, she looked down at her hands, ashamed she'd ever doubted whether she should have told him.

A brief moment of silence passed between them, but for Zoey, it felt like hours. Finally, the Director spoke once more.

"And what about today?"

With no hesitation, she spilled every detail about her plan and how she'd written Jemma a note. She told him about the entire conversation about the Shadow Dynasty, every detail about the Director they'd given her. He looked at her appraisingly.

"The adhesive listening devices. I didn't send the prototype to the Board. I put it in your ring before giving it to you this morning. On Friday, I knew something was off, but I chalked it up to stress and a sense of disconnection. But it was nagging at me all weekend, so I gave myself an insurance policy. Seems I was right to doubt you."

Zoey looked at the ring on her left hand, then raised her eyes to look at the Director.

"I promise, I wasn't trying to hide it from you for any other reason than I'd been sloppy. I was just trying to cover myself."

"If I *ever* think, even for one second, that you've removed that device or taken the ring off your finger while you're in the field, you will spend every moment of the rest of your life regretting it."

Three things. There's always something else. Something more.

"Yes, sir."

"When you return in the evenings, you will immediately deliver the ring to me. I will ensure you have it before you leave it in the mornings."

"Yes, sir."

"Defy me again, Zoey, and it will be the last thing you do here at DNP."

"Yes, sir." She spoke loudly and clearly, but fear was destroying her on the inside.

"Go to your cabin. I'll let you know if I decide to allow you to eat dinner tonight."

"Yes, sir." Zoey left, hoping to get as far away as possible before he decided to hurt her again.

DIRECTOR

Something in him had snapped when he found out Zoey had lied to him. Managing her used to just be part of the job, but now he found himself enjoying taking his anger out on her. She had begged him for mercy, which meant he now had complete control over Zoey. This was different from the simulation at Camp, too. There, a part of her had to know a stopping point existed. But now, he could use his weapon against her at any time, for any reason, and there was nothing she could do about it. He found himself almost wanting to press that small button again, just for the sake of it. Their testing indicated he could use the weapon within a ten-mile range- a range which he had the team working to increase. Ultimately, he wanted the device to be able to work anywhere he decided to send Zoey, but he had to be careful about moving forward that way. Many at DNP weren't aware of the Board's true plans.

The Board. I need to fill them in on the Maxwells.

The Director tapped out an email on his laptop, indicating that he was headed over to provide an update. They would be angry, of course, that Zoey had been told about the Shadow Dynasty, but all was not lost. She still didn't seem to believe it, so they had a few options. They could continue pushing her to believe the Maxwells were using drugs, a possibility supplied by Zoey herself. For all he cared, they could tell her the Dynasty was real. She didn't have to know their real plans and he knew he had finally stamped the fight out of her.

He spoke to no one as he made his way to the garage, where an attendant called for his customary vehicle. He didn't even acknowledge the driver other than to tell him he had a meeting with the Board. His thoughts were focused solely on Zoey's pathetic display and how he couldn't wait for the next opportunity to break her some more.

DIRECTOR

You have to pull her from the field before she becomes an even bigger liability.

The Board had not taken the news well, but the Director didn't flinch at their anger. He knew he'd done the job they'd set before him.

"If you wish for me to pull her, that's fine. But you should know that there's no chance Zoey will turn on DNP or me now."

She's been under your watch for twenty-one years. Why should we believe she will give you absolute deference now?

So, he told them that he'd injected her with a GPS device, that he'd lied to her about not being able to remove the interrogation chip, and that he'd used it against her. The Director didn't mention that her lies had caused him to use it because that wasn't relevant anymore. Everyone had the same information, and now they knew he was willing to do whatever it took to accomplish their goals. He even recounted with glee the agony he'd caused and her desperation for his pardon.

"She'll do anything for me now."

Then perhaps it's time she met The Board. Have someone plant evidence of drugs around the Maxwells to bolster that story with her.

"Of course. When would you like to meet her?"

Tonight. We don't want to send her back in until we have destroyed any possibility she might believe the Maxwells.

"I'll return with her this evening."

ZOEY

Safely back in her cabin (as safe as she could feel given the circumstances), Zoey curled into a tight ball in the corner of her couch, wrapped in a blanket. She allowed herself to cry as many tears as she could for about five minutes, then pulled herself together. So many thoughts were racing through her mind.

This is just a coincidence. He's mad because I hid things from him, but he's not the monster that Jemma and Todd claim he is. He would never actively try to keep me under the control of some evil organization. That's just crazy. I deserved all of it, anyway. None of what just happened would have happened if I'd told him everything from the start.

Her stomach rumbled in pain, and she did her best to push away the discomfort. She didn't anticipate she would be receiving much, if anything for dinner. It didn't matter, really. Despite her body's current protest, the last thing she wanted to do was eat. All she really wanted to do was focus on doing her job and doing it well, making sure that the Director never had reason to be angry with her again.

Zoey forced herself off the couch, determined to take a shower and get her head back in the game.

The piping hot water soothed her and allowed her to relieve some of the tension she'd been holding in her body. She hadn't even realized how bad that had been until she began loosening up, realizing how sore she felt. As she scrubbed the already runny makeup off her face, she heard the door to her cabin open. No agents had access to any other agent's cabin, which meant it could only be the Director. Zoey did her best to wrap up quickly. Once dry, she slipped into a pair of black leggings and an oversized maroon sweater- it was what she'd planned to sleep in that evening.

When she walked back into the main room of the cabin, she noticed the Director sitting at the small table, flipping through a notebook. No, not a notebook. That was her sketchbook. She froze, unsure what to do. She'd never shown him any of her art before and she'd often used sketching as a type of journaling. His eyes lifted to her, almost surprised.

"I didn't know you could draw." His voice had no emotion.

"I just do it every now and then."

"These are good."

She hesitated, unable to keep up with his ever-changing moods.

"Thank you."

He ripped a drawing out of the sketchbook before closing it and sliding it to his side on the table, then folded the single page and placed it in his pocket. *Which sketch did he take? Why would he do that?*

Zoey remained standing where she was, not willing to say a word to him about his theft. For a moment, she thought he might even be trying to bait her into reacting, but she was too afraid to do so after what had happened.

"You're going to need to change clothes."

"Why? I mean, I will. Where am I going? I mean, I'm not questioning it. I just don't know how I should dress?" She stumbled over her words, stupefied at her inability to put together a complete sentence. The Director seemed almost amused though and she could have sworn she saw a hint of a smirk on his face.

"I'd recommend something nice but understated. You don't want to give The Board any wrong impressions."
Her jaw dropped. *Did he just say...*

"The Board?" she squeaked. *I sound so pathetic right now.*

"Yes, Zoey, The Board. They'd like to meet with you, preferably tonight, so if you wouldn't mind hurrying it along..."

"Yes, sir." The *last* thing Zoey wanted to do was keep The Board waiting. She could barely handle an angry Director; no way would she let herself get on their bad side as well. She grabbed a black pantsuit with faint white pinstripes and changed in the bathroom, applying minimal makeup and brushing out her hair. Checking in the mirror, she realized she didn't even recognize herself. All she saw staring back at her was a girl with lifeless eyes and a too-thin face. She looked fragile, not at all like the first-class agent she knew herself to be. Not wanting to linger over the thoughts, she went back to the closet and put on a pair of low heels then returned to stand before the Director.

"That suit looks nice on you."

"Thank you."

For a moment he looked like might say something else, but instead he let out a deep breath before motioning for her to follow him. When he turned, she stole one last curious glance at her sketchbook before leaving the cabin.

ZOEY

The last time Zoey was at the Board's offices was when the Director had first found her in that alley when she was nine. She hadn't met the Board back then but remembered how imposing the building had been. She found herself walking nervously behind the Director as they approached the building's entrance. He didn't seem to notice she'd fallen a couple paces behind until he reached the door, then looked impatiently at her while waiting for her to catch up.

"I strongly recommend that you be on your very best behavior during this meeting, Zoey." She had already planned on it but couldn't help but hear the underlying threat in his voice. She wondered if he would use the weapon on her on the spot, in front of these mysterious people who influenced her entire world.

"Yes, sir."

As they stood outside the doors to the boardroom where business was conducted, Zoey could almost see her younger self, sitting on the bench and kicking her feet. Seeming to read her mind, the Director moved closer to her.

"If I had to go back in time, I still would have brought you in with me that night. I still would have saved you."

A lump formed in her throat, rendering her unable to respond with anything other than a gentle nod. *This is why they're wrong. He wouldn't say things like that if he was trying to hurt me. The stuff earlier today, that was because of my decisions, my actions. He didn't want to do that.*

The door to the boardroom appeared to open on its own and the Director gestured for Zoey to step inside before him, straightening his tie as she walked past. *Guess he wants to be on his best behavior too.*

She felt the Director's grip on her left elbow, steering her to a spot in the center of the room. They stood next to each other, arms at their sides, looking straight forward as a group of nine individuals entered from a door to the left and took seats in front of them. *No one said this would be like standing in front of the Supreme Court or something.*

One of the Board members, a woman who appeared to be in her mid-fifties if Zoey had to guess, spoke first.

Good evening, Zoey. It's wonderful to finally meet you in person.

Zoey was taken aback by her pleasant tone and took a beat too long to respond, judging by the way the Director cut his eyes sideways at her.

"Good evening. It's nice to meet all of you as well."

Typically, we do not meet with agents or other DNP employees. As I'm sure you are aware, we find it easier to funnel our directions through the

Director. We understand your current assignment, however, has provided you with rather...interesting theories on who we are and thought it best to clear up any questions once and for all.

Zoey blinked a few times then turned toward the Director, looking for any indication of what she was supposed to do now. *Surely he wouldn't want me to interrogate them? Is this a trick?*

I'm speaking directly to you, Zoey. The Director has no intention of interfering in our conversation.

She felt him stiffen slightly beside her. *So, he doesn't love being told what to do, either.*

"I don't exactly know what to say, ma'am." *Not a question, still respectful.*

Surely you'd like to discuss this notion of a Shadow Dynasty? Several of the Board members chuckled; others rolled their eyes at the words.

"Honestly, ma'am, that sounded a little farfetched to me. It felt more like they were trying everything they could to turn me against DNP, and that theory was the best they could come up with at the time."

Have they been successful? Are you considering leaving DNP?

"No, ma'am, I've honestly never thought about going to another agency."

That's not the question she asked. Another Board member spoke up, an imposing man at the far end of the table, closest to the door through which they'd all entered.

Have you considered leaving DNP at all?

"Not in any actionable way." *Why didn't I just say no? Seriously, what is wrong with me?* She could tell the Director wondered the same thing, even though he made no movements and remained quiet. The man on the Board spoke again.

What does "not in any actionable way" mean?

"Forgive me, I don't think that's actually the word I was looking for at the moment. I just meant, of course I've thought about what life would be like if I retired one day or something like that, but I haven't just outright made any plans to leave. Sir." She added the "sir" hastily, desperate to keep this meeting from going off the rails.

Who doesn't dream of a peaceful retirement? The first lady spoke again, a small smile on her face. **Tell us, Zoey. How do you think the Maxwells figured out that you were undercover?**

Zoey paused, frowning slightly. They hadn't really given a satisfactory response to that the last time they spoke. *What did they say? "You fell into our laps." But how did they know?*

"Actually, ma'am, I'm not sure. When Jemma was telling me that the Director worked for the Shadow Dynasty, she said she didn't know who he was trying to recruit until I fell into their laps. Before I had time to push that any further, Todd indicated he was going to force me to join them, so I went into fight mode."

Would he have succeeded?

She snorted a laugh, quickly covering it as a cough as best she could before things went completely sideways.

"I doubt it. I've never seen him fight before, but I'm pretty sure he hasn't had any formal training. Jemma said they hadn't even considered starting a new company until..."

Until?

Did the Director play the recording for them? Am I about to tell them something they don't already know? It doesn't matter, I guess. I have to answer.

"She said that you, er, the Shadow Dynasty, tried to recruit them and they didn't want to join."

At one point, we believed that their combined prowess in the financial market may have benefited some of our governmental contract work, but we were unwilling to pay them the salaries they requested.

"Oh wait. That's probably it then, right? They are calling you the Shadow Dynasty because a lot of work we do is in secret? I mean, it's a dumb name but at least that explains how they came up with it, especially if they were unhappy with the offer you made."

Everyone stared at her for a moment, including the Director. *Oh come on, this can't be a reach?*

That...is very possible, Zoey, thank you for the assessment. We question whether it makes sense to send you back to Mirror Bank tomorrow, considering you have no real cover anymore, but we are interested in finding out how the Maxwells determined you were an agent for DNP. What are your thoughts on returning?

Of all the answers she could have given, she picked the one she firmly believed was mostly likely to meet the Director's approval.

"My job is to follow orders, ma'am. Whatever the Director and the Board believe is best, I'll do as requested."

This time the man spoke again.

That's very good to hear, Zoey. Very good. We will discuss the options and let you know, Director, before 0600 tomorrow.

"Yes, sir," the Director said, slightly bowing his head. *Woah. Did he just say, sir?*

The woman wished them well and the Board members left the room. Once they had all filed through the door, the Director again grabbed Zoey by the elbow, directing her out of the building.

"Not a word until we're back at headquarters, understood?" He whispered into her ear.

She nodded and got into the waiting vehicle and spent the ride back terrified that she'd done something horribly wrong.

DIRECTOR

The Director sat still and quiet as possible for the duration of the ride back to headquarters. Being so close to the Board and their power always impacted him, and it was stronger this time with all the force they put into disguising themselves as people. He himself felt drained, as if they'd been pulling on the magick they'd imbibed in him so that he could maintain his human form. He wondered how the meeting might have impacted Zoey, then, as she was the first mortal he'd ever brought directly to them.

As they got closer to headquarters, the fog around him seemed to clear and he was once more comfortable in his disguise. He knew she'd been planning on sleeping before he went to her cabin earlier and that she was severely weakened from her punishment, but he wanted to regain his position of power with her after showing subservience to the Board, so he beckoned her to follow him to his office.

"You understand the gravity of what just happened, don't you? Sit down." As he had been about to sit behind his desk, he noticed she was eyeing him warily and that she looked like she might collapse.

As she gingerly lowered herself into the seat, she replied.

"Do I understand that the Board demanded my presence to determine whether I'd been compromised? Yes, sir."

He wanted to grin. *So, she has been listening to me all these years. She does understand the chain of command. She is thinking the way we want her to think.*

"And do you believe you were able to convince them?"

"Honestly, I'm more concerned about whether I convinced you."

He was surprised. *Surely she knows my opinion means nothing if it differs from that of the Board. But...she values my opinion. She needs my approval.*

"I believe you aren't planning to defect to another agency. Though I was surprised to hear that at only thirty you've been considering retirement."

"Eventually, sir. Not today . . ." her voice trailed though, and he knew she wasn't being completely honest, but he'd pushed her enough today.

"For what it's worth, I do think they believed you. I'm not sure what they are going to decide as far as sending you back in tomorrow, but I recommend you follow the lights out protocol this evening just in case."

"Yes, sir." She stood, letting her eyes focus on the pocket where he'd earlier placed one of her sketches.

"You may go, Zoey." He watched as her attention returned to him before leaving his office.

Once she was gone, he settled back into his seat, replaying the meeting in his mind. It really had gone better than he could have hoped for considering her typical inability to keep her mouth shut or know when to stop. A call to his office line broke his train of thought.

"Yes?"

"The job is done, sir. We used cocaine."

"You weren't seen?"

"No, sir."

"Good."

He hung up the line and fished the drawing from his pocket. It showed the dark alley where he "found" Zoey, and his mind took him back to the night he'd killed her parents.

DIRECTOR

The Board had been frustrated with him for months, threatening to shut down his position as Director because he had not had any long-term success in recruiting for them. Agents came and went like DNP was a set of revolving doors. They always needed him when he found them, but none were willing to give themselves fully over to him. He couldn't break them down the way he needed to in order to provide them to the Board, the Shadow Dynasty, as new Knight Mares. And as a Knight Mare himself, that was his only job-to groom new Knight Mares. For some reason though, each of his recruits drew on an inner strength and fought back before he could fully envelop them into the Dynasty's world.

Agitated at his recurring failures, he slipped back into his true form to prowl for potential recruits to the Shadow cause. As he made his way through the crowds of people walking from shop to shop on a busy street, he heard arguing. When he found the source, he noticed a couple bickering over whose turn it was to spend time with their small child, each one trying to push her off on the other. The girl gazed around, and, for a brief moment, it seemed as though she could see him. He had to shake away the thought. Knight Mares weren't visible to mortals unless *disguised. All the same, it felt as though she was looking straight at him.*

Soon after, she turned around to see her parents had walked on continuing their argument, not bothering to notice she was no longer with them. A man approached the girl and asked if she was lost, and the Director watched as she stopped on the man's foot with all her might before storming after her family.

Finally, he'd found the perfect target. Children could be more easily manipulated than adults and, in the meantime, he could provide her with a better life than she would ever have with her mother and father, judging by the looks of them. As the day grew darker, he began sending his Whispers. They pushed and pulled on the family as if they were not more than a strong wind all while guiding them to a secluded alley. Once there, the Director pushed the Whispers to surround them all, both singularly and as a group, obscuring their senses of sight and sound. He began feeding the child a new reality. She was too much to handle and her parents couldn't stand her. She was always in their way, keeping them from living the way they'd always wanted. He pushed and pushed until the girl was on her knees in the mud, tears streaming down her face. Then, he ate her parents' souls and minds, taking every memory they'd ever had of the child-Zoey-before allowing the Whispers to dispose of their bodies.

The darkness settled and the sounds of the streets behind them returned, as the Director approached Zoey from behind, masked by his human form.

"Are you okay? Please, please let me help you, Zoey."

And the crying child allowed him to lift her off the ground and carry her to the boardroom, where her life would change forever.

ZOEY

Zoey rocketed upright in her bed, hardly able to breathe, sweat pouring from every inch of her body. She hadn't had bad dreams about her parents leaving her during that terrible storm in a long time.

It's just because I figured out which sketch he took. She willed her heart rate to lower itself as she allowed her thoughts to return to that night, though she didn't remember much. She knew she'd been out with her parents for the day and that they had been fighting nonstop but, then again, that had been nothing new to her. The next thing she knew she was on the ground in that alley and the Director was approaching her, trying to soothe her. He'd never told her much about that day, either. When she was younger, she'd asked a couple times, but he always just told her that he happened to be passing by on his way to meet with the Board when he saw her there, alone.

The clock beside her bed told Zoey it was four in the morning. Too early to get ready for the bank, if she was even going, but too late to fall back asleep and get any real rest. Zoey got out of bed and made some coffee. Apparently, the Director had no intention of confiscating that from her, as he had everything else that had been in her now empty kitchen when she first angered him several weeks ago. Once she had a hot, fresh cup of coffee in her hands she walked to the couch, sitting once more under a blanket in the corner.

We heard something telling us to go that way.

Zoey almost dropped the full mug in surprise as the thought entered her mind. *No, that's just part of the dream this time. It's always a little bit different. But…I've heard those voices since then.*

They weren't really voices though, more thoughts that intruded into her mind. She had always chalked it up to being tired from work or from lack of sleep, and she had never mentioned it to anyone. The Director would have never put her on another assignment if he thought she was hearing things and she didn't want to risk being locked underground forever. She needed missions in order to survive.

A knock came at the door and Zoey commanded the AI to allow it to slide open, surprised to see the Director standing there waiting, especially after he'd just let himself in several hours before. She started to move her blanket so she could stand, but he waved at her to remain sitting and joined her at the other end of the couch.

"The Board wants you to return to Mirror Bank today to see if you can get any more information on how the Maxwells determined you were a DNP agent. We are going to give you a ride, though, so that if things go sideways, we can pull you out quickly."

He eyed the black coffee in her hands.

"Go to the dining hall and eat something. I don't really care what you get either, but make sure you get something somewhat substantial. If Todd

Maxwell really tries to start a fight with you then you'll need more energy than what that coffee is giving you to stand a chance against him."

The thought that she no longer even felt hungry entered her mind, but she quickly pushed it away. *It's that weird voice again.*

"Yes, sir," she responded but she didn't move. For a brief moment, she wondered whether she actually could. By this point, both her body and mind were so exhausted, so weakened, that she could barely take care of herself. Apparently, the Director wondered the same thing because he stood, taking Zoey's coffee mug and setting it on the table in front of them, then extended his arm to help her rise.

Chivalrous.

Zoey weakly grabbed his arm and pulled herself up, noting that he was actually the one doing most of the pulling.

"Thank you." Her voice barely audible as the room began spinning around her.

"Zoey!" The Director barked at her as if she'd been ignoring him and the room came back into focus.

"What just happened, Zoey?"

"Nothing, I'm just a little tired still." And she turned away to find something in her closet to wear.

"Be in the dining hall in ten minutes, Zoey. I mean it."

"Yes, sir."

He left, and she got dressed and ready for her final foray at Mirror Bank.

ZOEY

The dining hall was fairly empty when Zoey arrived. It would probably be another hour or so before others started filtering in, but she didn't mind. The quiet gave her time to focus her thoughts on the day rather than on the dream that so startlingly woke her. She sat at one of the smaller tables on the far side of the room, picking at her food. She'd gotten a full breakfast of eggs, sausage, a biscuit and gravy, and two glasses of orange juice, but was finding it difficult to eat much of it. She forced down as much as she could, though, certain the agent sitting across the room with a book and full plate in front of him was acting as the Director's eyes. When she felt like she'd eaten at least enough to not be in trouble, she made her way up to the outdoor area and sat at the bench facing the water fountain.

The Director hadn't requested to meet with her there, but today felt different to her. Maybe it was because she didn't have a real cover anymore and was just going to have to hope that the Maxwells were still interested enough in recruiting her that they would give her more answers but, whatever it was, her gut feeling told her that a major shift in her life was coming. The Board had obviously decided she was a trustworthy agent, which was a huge deal in her mind. *Maybe I'll get a promotion or something.* A quick breeze on an otherwise still day ruffled her hair. As she reached up to tuck the flyaway strands back behind her ear, she heard a voice from behind her.

"I didn't expect to find you here."

Really, she'd known he had been there before the words came out of his mouth. She almost always felt the winds change when he snuck up on her. *Okay well that's just my imagination going a little crazy. I probably heard him step on a leaf or something.*

"I had a few minutes to kill and didn't want to go back to my cabin." She didn't move as he sat next to her on the bench, holding out the box containing the fake engagement ring. Zoey took the box but didn't open it to put the ring on right away. She needed a few more moments before she would be ready for the task set before her.

"They are going to try to take you today."

"I know." Her eyes remained focused on the fountain, watching water splash into the pool at the bottom.

"Don't let them." He almost whispered the words, as if the idea pained him to his very core.

She turned to him, giving him a half smile.

"I'm not the kind of girl who makes life easy for people." The Director chuckled.

"No, no you're not."

They sat together in silence for a few more moments, enjoying the peaceful atmosphere surrounding them, unsure whether they'd be afforded the same luxury again the next morning, or any morning after. Then the Director stood, and Zoey followed suit, putting the ring on her finger and handing the box back to him.

DIRECTOR

Everyone was tense as the three SUVs made their way from headquarters to Mirror Bank. The Director had insisted Zoey ride with him. He would drop her off a safe enough distance from the bank so that no one would see her getting out of the convoy, but he refused to let her out of his sight a moment too soon.

The Board had stressed for the better part of an hour how imperative it was that he not let anything happen to their soon-to-be newest Knight Mare. Apparently, she had behaved well enough last night that they were ready to heap praise on the Director for his good work. Now the pressure was on him, though, to keep things from going south in a hurry. Sure, Zoey was a highly skilled agent. But no one knew how well-trained Jemma or Todd were or what they had in the way of resources. He certainly suspected they had more assistance nearby than Edna, but they'd done nothing to lead him to those resources. The surveillance team who had been assigned to trail them ever since Zoey's cover started hadn't been able to uncover anything. That's really what worried him most about this situation-if they were that good at hiding, then they were dangerous.

He had to rein it in though because he could tell his tension was impacting Zoey. She hadn't said anything since they'd gotten in the vehicle, but she was popping her knuckles repeatedly, a habit he hated but also a tell-tale sign of her anxiety.

"Stop doing that." He snapped a little too harshly at her and she quit immediately, laying her hands flat on her thighs just above her knees.
"You're going to get yourself too worked up to pay attention to your surroundings if you're not careful."

"Yes, sir."

He adjusted his sunglasses before continuing.

"You remember the plan? Everything we discussed?"

"Yes, sir."

"Anything else you can think of that might help? Anything you might have noticed?"

"No, sir."

A stillness fell over them briefly and Zoey turned to look at him.

"Did you bring it with you?"

"Did I bring what with me?"

"The control device."

This time he took his sunglasses off completely as he looked searchingly into her eyes.

"The control device?"

"For the interrogation chip."

"Zoey, I swear if you are planning to do something-"

"I'm not. I just…if something goes wrong and it sounds like they might overpower me or try to move me, use it."

"Why would I do that? You're weak enough already, I would just be handing you to them."

"You don't get it. I can't fight that thing. I react every time. I fall, I scream. If you use it while they are with me, it will absolutely cause a scene. It will make it easier for you to pull me out if everyone is trying to figure out what they are doing to me."

He was stunned. *Here she is, going into a dangerous situation with people promising her a different world, a better world, and she would rather live through that agony again than to leave me.*

"Zoey," but she cut him off.

"Just promise, if something happens and there's a chance it will help, you'll use it."

He wanted to reprimand her for giving him orders but he couldn't bring himself to do it after his realization.

"Fine. But if I use it, I'm not going to take it easy on you."

"I wouldn't expect you to, sir."

They pulled into a small parking lot a few blocks from the bank. As Zoey climbed out, he leaned toward her.

"Let's get this over with so we can move on from the Maxwells."

"Yes, sir," she replied, smirking as she gave a half cocky salute before slamming the door and walking away.

CTRL + Z

I'm going to make her regret asking me to use the device.

ZOEY

"How did you know I worked for DNP?"

Zoey wasted no time pushing into Todd's office where he and Jemma sat, enjoying a cup of coffee. Todd jumped slightly as she entered, causing him to spill coffee on his desk.

"Zo-Katie, we should have this conversation elsewhere, don't you think?" The alarm on Jemma's face was almost palpable.

"I'm not wearing my earpiece today. In fact, I'm not even supposed to be here. But my cover has *never* been blown in all the time I've been an agent, so answer my question. How did you know?" She pushed as much force through her voice as she could muster.

"We explained to you that-"

"No. No you didn't. You didn't explain anything. You said you were trying to find DNP's next target or whatever you think the Board is doing and that I 'fell in your laps,' but that doesn't explain how you made the connection."

All those years of watching the Director get really mad at me are starting to pay off, I guess. They look so worried.

"Please, calm down, and let me explain then, okay?" The humor wasn't lost on Zoey as Jemma raised her hands like she was trying to talk down a bank robber. Todd, however, started to move toward the front of his desk.

"Stop! Sit at your desk chair and don't move an inch toward me. I want answers, Todd, not a fight, but I'll take you out if I have to."

Keeping one hand up in front Zoey, Jemma used the other to motion Todd back to his seat, where he went reluctantly. Zoey looked back at Jemma expectantly.

"Remember I told you that the Shadow Dynasty wanted-"

"I met the Board, Jemma. They aren't creepy shadow creatures; they are just people. Maybe you were weirded out by their intensity or whatever, but I don't want to hear any more about shadows. Tell me how you knew I worked for DNP and stop wasting time."

Jemma sighed but continued. "The Dynasty, the *Board*, wanted us to form another branch of DNP. To become Directors at other locations. But we weren't willing to do the things required of someone to become a Director, so we walked away. We know what they require of Directors though, Zoey, and we had met your Director before. Did he tell you that? Did you know that he knows us personally?"

"I'm running out of patience, Jemma." She refused to let them know that information had thrown her.

"We knew we had to watch him so…so we…"

"That's enough, Jemma." Todd stood once more. "If we give her any more information, we *have* to extract her immediately. We can't risk her going back and telling the Director any of this."

"She'll never come with us willingly if we don't give her answers."

"She's not going to come with us willingly regardless."

"If we forcibly extract her she won't trust us. If we give her some details first maybe she'll be able to come around though. It's the only way we can help her."

"Both of you stop talking like I'm not in the room. I'm not going anywhere by will or force, but if you don't answer my question right now, *I'm* going to resort to violence."

"We put someone inside DNP, Zoey. Someone who could help us weed through all the agents and figure out who the Director would bring in next. We never considered you in all the information our source sent over because you'd been there so long. But when we found out DNP was sending you here to look into us, it was all that made sense."

"Who is it?" She ground out through clenched teeth, but Todd jumped in before Jemma could answer.

"You're going to come with us now, Zoey. If I have to knock you unconscious to take you I will, but you're coming with us. We have to get you away from here before DNP starts looking for you, if they aren't already."

"DNP knows where I am."

Jemma inhaled sharply. "You said you weren't supposed to be here."

"You said creepy magic people controlled my life. We're even on lies then, right?"

"They won't know where she is for long, Jemma, we just have to get her out of here. Now."

"Even if you thought you could overpower me, Todd, DNP would still find me with ease."

"Even if that GPS tracker injected in you had been disabled?"

She looked squarely at Todd, finally putting the pieces together.

"Trevor."

"We can't let you tell the Director, Zoey. Trevor will be tortured and terminated. You're coming with us." He lunged forward and grabbed Zoey's wrist, but she was fast enough to twist away before he could tighten his grip.

She wrenched the door open and began running through the still mostly empty hallways, trying to reach the back exit, but her speed and endurance had waned, and Todd tackled her from behind. She attempted to free herself while he tried to restrain her wrists behind her back with his necktie and managed to elbow him in the jaw. Zoey scrambled to crawl away from him, but his weight was so heavy on top of her almost emaciated body that he quickly pinned her in place before once again working to restrain her. Fortunately, Zoey had made it close enough to the back door to see other employees headed their way. No doubt Todd and Jemma would say she stole something once they witnessed the chaotic scene in the hallway, but Zoey refused to let them win that easily.

"NOW! Do it RIGHT NOW!" She yelled, obviously confusing Todd, who stilled briefly.

"What?"

"I said do it NOW!" And she knew the Director got the message because an inescapable pain began tearing through her body, forcing her to scream and convulse in agony.

Todd jumped off her and Jemma ran forward, trying to see what happened. The pain stopped momentarily, and tears flooded Zoey's eyes as she gasped for breath. She could hear the door opening, indicating the entrance of other employees.

"Again, you have to do it again," she could barely get the words out, but they found their listener as the pain kicked back into full gear.

"Someone help! Make them stop, get them away from me! Help!" She reached her arms out to the entering employees who looked bewildered. Jemma immediately jumped back toward Todd, fumbling over her words as she tried to explain the situation away.

As the pain faded once more, Zoey took the opportunity to drag herself to her feet and push forward toward the door, pleading with everyone to let her by, to escape the Maxwells.

"They are crazy, keep them away please! I have to get out of here! Please help!"

One young man grabbed hold of her and helped her exit the bank, trying desperately to find out what happened. Zoey kept crying and mumbled incoherently before using every bit of strength she had remaining to break free and run down the street, Todd's tie dangling from her wrist. By the time Jemma and Todd got through the crowd and parking lot, she had already rounded a corner and was far out of sight. The Director's vehicle flew up next to her and she felt him grabbing her and lifting her inside while the driver sped away.

"Trevor-" she panted.

"We will handle him."

"No, he probably has the GPS control. All he has to do is turn it on and help them find me the next time I'm on assignment."

The Director called someone in medical to tell them to prepare to remove the implanted tracker then threw his phone down into the floorboard.

"Are you hurt?"

"No- just have to..." she still hadn't caught her breath, "have to recover from the device. You didn't have to let it go so long the first time..."

"I wasn't sure, we didn't have a chance to discuss signals when you decided to give *me* orders."

Oh.

Sirens sounded and Zoey saw a flood of flashing blue lights headed toward Mirror Bank. The Director leaned forward and turned on a local police scanner, and the two listened as reports came through of notorious drug dealers Jemma and Todd Maxwell being arrested for possession of a large amount of cocaine in their vehicle, which was searched after reports they had attacked a young employee at the bank. Speculation was that she had caught them setting up a major deal that morning and they tried to take her out of the picture. Katie Charles was now missing, and police were combing the immediate area to try to get her to safety.

"Cocaine. No wonder they thought the Board was a group of spooky demons." And then Zoey passed out, falling over onto the Director.

DIRECTOR

"GET OUT OF THE WAY!"

The Director bellowed as he led the charge to the medtech wing, an agent carrying Zoey following closely behind him. Her breathing was labored, and her pulse was faint.

I wasn't supposed to kill her, just break her enough to make her Knight Mare. This can't be happening.

"Doctor, get over here." He said gruffly as Zoey was lowered onto a hospital style bed. The doctor and rest of the medical staff pushed him out of the room as they got to work on her, trying to bring her back into consciousness.

The Director couldn't bear the thought of reporting to the Board without knowing if she could be stabilized, partially for fear of their anger and partially because he was genuinely concerned for her well-being. He gripped Todd Maxwell's tie tightly- he'd ripped it off Zoey's arm after she passed out on the way to headquarters. He was furious that the Maxwells thought they could just steal Zoey from him, as if they had any right to her.

"Director?"

"What?" He snapped; his eyes narrowed at the agent who had interrupted his thoughts.

"Sir, we do have Trevor in our custody. A security member saw him leaving with a box full of equipment and stopped him right before your order to detain him came in, so he wasn't able to get anything out of the building."

"Good. Go keep an eye on him. No one talks to him before I do."

"Yes, sir." The agent scurried off, not wanting to risk the Director's wrath.

I should have him injected with one of the interrogation chips. There's no way he could withstand it; not considering the effect it has on Zoey. I wonder if she would want to be the one to torture him for information. I think I could enjoy watching that. Surely she's angry enough that he put her in danger. Even if she doesn't want to, I could order her to do it. Tell her it's what the Board wants. She does need to learn how to demand information and force action if she's going to be promoted soon.

He continued pacing, getting more infuriated with each passing moment. He knew he hadn't overdone the pain administration; he'd used it at a higher level for a longer period and more times in a row during the simulation. But he *had* noticed how weak Zoey looked that morning. He allowed his frustration to blame Zoey for her ridiculous idea to use the device in the first place. She always had a flair for the dramatics, and he frequently had to talk her into more reasonable methods. There just hadn't been time to come up with another option this morning. *She purposely waited until we were almost to the bank to hit me with that plan.*

Then another thought occurred to him. *Did the Maxwells notice what was going on in that moment? Did they think she was just acting, or did they realize she was in actual pain? How much information was Trevor able to pass to them? He couldn't have told them about the device. But Todd did say Zoey would never go willingly. I wonder if he thought she would be concerned about me using it. No, he knew she was just loyal to me. She would never go willingly because she wouldn't want to.*

He was driving himself mad thinking of each random possibility and began to lose control over his disguise; he could feel himself shifting back into his Knight Mare form. Aware that the shift would cause a lot of questions he couldn't answer, he turned on his heels and left the waiting area, yelling to a nurse to come straight to his office when Zoey awoke. Once safely inside, he locked his door and allowed himself to fade into Knight Mare form and settled himself in the room, causing it to look as though he'd turned the lights out. The Director allowed himself to just be for a long while, before finally returning to human form. He sat at his desk and began plotting the demise of Jemma and Todd Maxwell.

ZOEY

The faint voices around her grew louder and louder and Zoey realized she had been taken to medtech, though she was unsure how long she'd been there. For a moment, she considered opening her eyes, but she could feel the bright overhead lights and opted to keep them shut for fear of worsening the already pounding headache she was experiencing. She listened as the doctors discussed her heart rate, which was apparently rising to a normal level. Air pushed in on her, and she realized she was wearing a mask that was feeding her oxygen, though she didn't feel like she needed it. She weakly reached a hand up to remove it, and someone gently grabbed her wrist to stop her.

"Zoey? Zoey, can you hear me?"

"You don't have to yell at me." She mumbled, each word causing additional throbbing through her head.

"Can you open your eyes?" the man said again, slightly gentler.

She opened them just a bit before squeezing them shut again.

"Could you turn the light off? It's too bright."

A few seconds later she could tell the lights were still on, but that they had at least been dimmed slightly. Slowly, she opened her eyes and had to blink several times for everyone around her to come into focus.

"Zoey, do you know where you are?" the voice asked again, and she realized it was Doctor Sanderson.

"I'm in medtech, and yes, I'm fine. Just a little headache. I'd like to go back to my cabin." Zoey made a feeble attempt to sit up but was quickly pushed back down onto the bed. She felt straps lock around her wrist. They were clearly concerned she would become agitated if they didn't let her leave but, if she was being honest with herself, she didn't have the energy to try to fight her way out in the first place.

"Just relax Zoey, we need to run some more tests and get that tracker out of you."

Zoey mumbled incoherently, not entirely sure herself what she was trying to say. Dr. Sanderson turned to one of the nurses and instructed her to tell the Director that Zoey was awake and stable, and that he would be able to see her soon.

She tried to remember how she'd gotten to medtech in the first place. She remembered Todd chasing her and the pain from the device. *I've got to see if I can bribe Doctor Sanderson into figuring out how to remove that too.* She recalled running through the bank crowd, the man who tried to help, and making it to the Director. She drew a blank on everything else after that.

Wait.

"Where's the tie?"

The chatter around her stopped and Doctor Sanderson stepped closer.

"What did you say?"

"The tie. The one that was on my wrist, where is it?"

"I believe the Director took it," an assistant in the back spoke up.

"Call him, tell him not to touch it again. I think someone did something to it when I was leaving...the...bank..."

Before she could finish explaining, her mind and body tired and she fainted once more.

This time when she awoke, she heard the Director talking to Doctor Sanderson.

"So, it was designed to take her out of commission for an extended period of time?"

"Yes, but I think he applied too high a dose. She's practically emaciated, so it's completely overwhelmed her system. I'm honestly surprised the remaining residue hasn't had any effect on you, Director. Are you sure we can't run a few tests just to make sure you're okay?"

"I'm fine Doctor and, like I said, if I sense any sort of reaction, I'll let you know immediately. If you're correct about the dosage level though, I wonder how Todd managed to avoid the interaction with it. He had to have had his hands all over the tie when he was trying to restrain Zoey."

"Because it wasn't on the tie then." The two men turned and looked at Zoey immediately, as if they'd been caught in a conversation they hadn't planned for her to overhear.

"What do you mean?" The Director asked, while Doctor Sanderson moved forward to poke and prod Zoey some more. He was shining a small flashlight into her eyes when she responded.

"It was the guy who tried to help me. Well, he pretended like he was trying to help me. He grabbed my arm like he was trying to help pull me through the crowd, but he definitely touched the tie. He must have been part of their backup we hadn't located yet."

"Zoey, can you take a few deep breaths for me?" Doctor Sanderson waved his stethoscope in her face, and she did as he asked.

"What guy? Who was he? Have you seen him before?"

"He was-"

"Just a few more deep breaths, please." Zoey scowled at Doctor Sanderson but didn't argue. Before letting her get back to her conversation with the Director, he ran through a series of questions to assess her condition and made her conduct a few memory tests. Once he was satisfied that all of her vitals were fully stabilized and she was unlikely to pass out again, he murmured something to the Director about her needing food and rest before giving them privacy to continue their discussion.

"How long was I out?"

"The first time or the second?" The Director said, his arms crossed as he leaned against the wall.

"Both?"

He sighed. "Seven hours the first time, then another three and a half."

"Ten and a half hours? They could have taken me almost anywhere in that time."

"I'm aware, which is why I need you to focus. Tell me about this guy who drugged you."

"I know I've seen him before; I just don't know where. Not at the bank. Maybe...the coffee shop! The day that they got me in that back room the first time, when I-"

"When you lied and said you'd just lost comms momentarily."

"When I pretended to have a breakdown in the coffee shop, he was in there."

She tried to avoid eye contact, noting he was still angry about her lying to him. *At least it's unlikely that he'll use the device again while I'm strapped to this hospital bed and hooked up to a million different monitors. Doctor Sanderson would have a fit.*

"Was he in line or was he sitting at a table?"

"He was sitting. I did see that he had a coffee and a pastry, and he had a book was listening to earbuds. I guess they were probably hooked up to Jemma and Todd like Edna's glasses, assuming that's really how she was able to hear what was going on at the bank. I guess Trevor took off this morning before we could find out how much he knows?"

"He tried, but someone noticed him carrying a box of his things. No termination order had gone out, so he was stopped as a matter of protocol. Just after that, they got my order to detain him if at all possible. He's sitting in interrogation room two now."

She wasn't able to suppress her shiver at the word "interrogation."

"How long will you make him wait?"

"At least until you're cleared to join me. I'll need you to listen to what he says and tell me if it matches with what you know about the Maxwells."

"If he says anything."

"You don't honestly think there's a possibility I won't get the information we need from him, do you?" The look in his eyes told her he expected only one answer.

"No, sir."

"I'll send someone up here with food soon so Doctor Sanderson doesn't go on a rampage, and I'll be arranging your meals again instead of letting you pick them, especially since you did such a poor job of that this morning."

I'm glad we're back to him chastising me as if I'm still a child.

"Yes, sir."

"Get some rest. I want you out of here as soon as possible."

"Yes, sir."

Zoey waited for the Director to leave then closed her eyes to rest a bit longer.

ZOEY

"Absolutely not."

Doctor Sanderson was wholly unimpressed with Zoey's declaration that she was fine and could return to her cabin for the evening.

"You're not leaving medtech for at least another day, longer if I can convince the Director."

"Seriously, I'm fine. I've eaten and you just said all my vitals were good. I just want to take a shower and get in my own bed."

"Which will turn into you going to the gym to work out your anger at the Maxwells or you staying up way past lights out or any one of the number of things you have a tendency to do. You're going to stay right here where I can keep an eye on you. I'll tighten those restraints up more if I have to."

Other than the Director, Doctor Sanderson was the one person at DNP who seemed to always get his way. A part of her hoped the Director would talk him down since Trevor was still waiting for questioning, but she doubted it. Aside from the Director's general glee at forcing her to obey orders she didn't want to, he also had pretty strict rules about all agents following medical directives. It made sense, given the high mental and physical levels with which they were required to perform. Even still, she planned to do her best to convince him to override Doctor Sanderson the next time he came by to check on her.

"If I promise I won't leave, will you take the restraints off so I can take a shower?"

"Are you expecting Prince Charming to show up here at headquarters for you?"

"I-wait. What?"

"Are you expecting him to come profess his love to you? Because if not, I can't think of a single reason you can't wait a while longer to take a shower."

"Ugh!!!" she groaned, pulling her arms up on the restraints in frustration, just as the Director entered the room, eyebrows raised.

"Oh now, here's your chance Zoey." Doctor Sanderson turned to the Director. "Before you let her get too far, just know that I'm not authorizing her to leave medtech tonight under any circumstances."

Zoey badly wanted to lunge at him but could only move her arms a few inches. He smiled at her and hummed as he walked over to tighten the restraints until she couldn't lift her arms at all.

"I'll be back to check your vitals again in a bit Zoey. If you need me before then you know you can just push that little button under your hand."

Cheerfully, he exited. She was just about to launch into her tirade when the Director held up a hand to stop her.

"The longer Trevor waits, the worse the anticipation gets. I want you out of here too, but

Doctor Sanderson is just going to keep prolonging releasing you the more you fight with him. So, stop and do what he tells you to do."

She slammed her head backwards into her pillow in frustration.

"I don't need to stay here."

"First you give me orders and now you're dispensing medical advice. You've managed to move up around here pretty quickly, all things considered."

His tone told her to discontinue her arguments immediately, but she wanted to try one last time.

"I swear I won't do anything other than sleep in my bed."

"Well, you can sleep just fine here so there's no real rush, is there?"

And that was it. She knew that if he hadn't given any indication of trying to jailbreak her by then, it was out of the question entirely. Pouting, she changed the subject.

"Were you able to find anything on the coffee shop guy?"

"We are working on it. The rest of the tech team isn't quite as fast as Trevor, so it's taking some time."

"So, I just have to lay here doing nothing to help figure out who he is until Doctor Sanderson takes pity on me?"

"I thought you just wanted to sleep in your own bed."

She glared at him before even realizing and was met with a matching glare. Neither one seemed interested in backing down, but Zoey knew there was no chance she was winning the standoff, so she finally looked away.

"Will you *please* at least try to get me out of here tomorrow afternoon? I hate feeling so useless."

"Do what Doctor Sanderson tells you to, Zoey. I don't want a report that you're giving him problems."

"Yes, sir."

At least he didn't say no.

DIRECTOR

"May I have a word, Doctor Sanderson?"

The Director beckoned for the head of the medical team to follow him down the hall to an empty spot.

"Realistically, how long do you need to observe her?"

"I'm not interested in arguing what's medically necessary for her, Director."

The Director held his hands out, indicating he wasn't trying to argue.

"I'm not questioning your judgment, Doctor. I'm genuinely asking you. I need to get an understanding of how serious her current condition is."

"Sorry, Director. I shouldn't have snapped. That girl just always seems to get herself into bad situations. Given how strong a reaction she had to the ointment, on top of her overall general state of health currently, I think we need to remain cautious until we are sure there won't be a regression. What time is it, 0300 on Wednesday morning?"

The Director nodded.

"Honestly, I can't see myself releasing her before Saturday morning and that's *if* she can follow directions."

"I can't wait much longer than that, Doctor. We have to start questioning Trevor soon and the Board will want Zoey back to work tracking down the Maxwells since they escaped."

"I'll do my best, Director. But if she destabilizes or anything changes, it may take longer."

"Is there anything I can do to help move things along?"

"Don't indulge her requests for release. And don't toy with her meals. I don't know how long you plan on keeping that up overall and it's none of my business, but she needs to eat healthfully, or her body won't heal."

"Why don't you handle meals while she's here in medtech? That way if you're not able to release her Friday morning, I can verify to the Board that we are doing everything we can."

"Sure, I'd prefer that."

"Call me if she gives you any trouble."

Doctor Sanderson laughed a bit before yresponding, "You might as well not go far away."

The Director shook his head. *Her reputation for rebellion is really out of hand.*

"You shouldn't have to call this time but if you do, I assure you, it will only be one time."

"You should get some rest yourself, Director. You'll be no good to any of us if you're not able to function yourself."

The Director thanked Doctor Sanderson for his concern and made his way through the residential wing, up the stairway to his above-ground home.

Rather than going straight to bed, he tossed his suit jacket over the arm of the couch and sat in his recliner. He'd be able to rest better if he dropped the disguise and returned to Knight Mare form, but his energy was so low he was concerned he wouldn't have the ability to return to the disguise if Doctor Sanderson called him.

A simple fix would be to go into town on a quick hunt. The local bars were still open so it wouldn't be hard for him to find someone putting off enough sadness or anger for him to feed on but that would put him out of contact completely. He weighed his options and decided he'd be less likely to face trouble with the Board if he fed, since that meant he would be better able to maintain control over the magick. Their rules on remaining in disguise around mortals they were working with were set in stone. Only once during his tenure with him had he heard of a Knight Mare slipping on that, and rumor was that they trapped him in his human form and took away all of his power before turning their back on him, forcing him to live a mortal life all alone.

So, the Director shifted and vanished from the home, zipping his way through the air toward Main Street. It didn't take him long to locate several potential targets. He could have fed on many of them, but he wanted to avoid drawing too much attention. If too many people went missing at once, the police would surely find their way to DNP, and he didn't have time to deal with the questions. Finally, he settled on one particularly lonely young man. He seemed to be in very good health overall which meant he would have a lot of energy to convert, and his sadness was mouthwatering. The Director sniffed the air around the man and picked up on his thoughts. Apparently, he'd just caught his fiancé out with another man, and he was heartbroken.

Excellent.

No one would be surprised that he took off after such an incident. The Director called for the Whispers, and they helped lure the inebriated man to a secluded area behind a nearly empty parking lot. He didn't really have the extra time, but he couldn't resist toying with him just a bit, so he had the Whispers tell him of his failures and remind him of how happy she had looked in the other man's arms. When tears started pouring from the man's eyes, he swooped in and swallowed his soul, leaving the mind behind. He didn't need those memories. He communicated to the Whispers to find a Knight Mare who wanted the mind before they feasted on the body. The last time Whispers took a mind, they had been unable to control their own power for days. After they consented, he returned to his home and easily transitioned back into the Director that everyone at DNP would recognize. He checked his cell phone and, to his relief, he hadn't missed any calls or messages. He let out a deep breath and got in bed, ready to let his human body rest.

ZOEY

"How am I supposed to eat breakfast if you're not going to loosen these restraints at all?"

"Sarah is going to help you eat."

"You mean she's going to feed me?" She asked, bewildered.

"Yes, so be nice to her."

"Why won't you let me feed myself?"

"Because after our late-night conversation, I don't trust you enough at the moment to not find some way to break out of here if I put slack in one of the restraints."

"What if I just refuse to eat then?"

"How well did that work out for you last time?" He turned toward her, and she realized he was almost as angry about that behavior as the Director had been.

"Okay, that was stupid to say. I'm sorry. But I swear I won't try to leave."

"How about we do it my way and if you can behave through breakfast and us getting that tracker out after, we can keep an open mind for lunch?"

Lunch? What, am I going to be stuck in medtech for the rest of my life?

"Okay," she said reluctantly, perturbed by the idea that someone was going to feed her as if she were a child. Sarah entered the room a few moments later carrying a tray of breakfast-a sliced banana, yogurt, cereal, and a glass of water.

"I didn't want to make your stomach hurt with anything too heavy," she smiled sweetly at Zoey, placing the tray on a small table next to Zoey's bed and settling in to feed her.

Zoey nodded, not able to speak through her embarrassment. Sarah set to work loading up spoonfuls to give Zoey, who took them without protest because Doctor Sanderson was still moving about the room, setting up equipment to remove the tracking device. A new wave of humiliation washed over her when the Director entered just as Sarah was feeding her a spoonful of yogurt. He actually looked shocked though, and Zoey could hear the agitation in his words as he spoke to Doctor Sanderson.

"I told you to take care of getting meals to her, not force-feed her while keeping her restrained." His eyes never left Zoey, which made her discomfort with the situation even worse.

"And I told her I'd remove the restraints before lunch if she could behave. She's actually done quite well."

"I'm really full, though." Zoey spoke up as Sarah lifted a spoonful of the cereal. Doctor Sanderson peered down at the tray.

"Yes, you've actually eaten more than I expected you to. We can hold off on more until lunch. Thank you, Sarah."

As much as she didn't want to, Zoey smiled feebly at Sarah and mouthed a "thanks." Sarah gathered up what little remained of the meal and left, most likely to return the tray to the dining hall.

"Zoey, I'm going to remove the restraint on your left wrist now so that you can turn onto your right side, and I can extract the tracking device. Do I have your word that you will not remove the right restraint, or will I need to tie down your left arm once you're on your side?"

"She won't fight you, Doctor."

The Director gave Zoey a look which she interpreted as a death threat just before Doctor Sanderson looked to her for confirmation.

"I won't try to remove it."

He didn't seem to fully believe her, but he released her left hand nonetheless. She flexed her hand slightly and gingerly rolled onto her right side without saying a word. She felt a cold metal disc press against her left shoulder blade, and Doctor Sanderson slowly moved it around until a beep sounded.

"Found it!" He marked a small spot on her upper back with a marker.

"Alright, Zoey, I'm going to use this" he held a cylindrical device in front of her face "to extract the tracker. You're going to feel a sharp sting as it opens your skin, and then you'll feel some small discomfort as the tracker is sucked out of your body."

"Any chance that would work on our favorite new interrogation chip too?"

"Zoey." The Director warned her, and she didn't say another word. She could certainly be happy enough about having the tracker removed, and she was determined not to give the Director a reason to use the other device anyway. A sharp stabbing pain shot through Zoey's body, and she gripped the rail in front of her to keep herself from punching Doctor Sanderson with her free arm.

"That was more than just 'small discomfort'," she said through gritted teeth.

"Well, you're fine and the tracker is gone, so no reason to dwell on it." Doctor Sanderson spoke as he cleaned up the blood around the site where the tracker was pulled from her body and bandaged it.

"You can turn back over now."

So, she rolled back and sighed, presenting her left arm to him so he could reattach the restraint.

"You really *have* done a number on her, haven't you?" He said to the Director, who looked annoyed at the comment.

"I think she's proven the restraints are no longer necessary, Doctor."

"I agree."

Before Doctor Sanderson could round the bed, the Director was already there, releasing Zoey's other arm. Relief poured from her as she could finally use her arms to adjust herself in the bed, sitting upright on her own.

"Don't think that means you're going anywhere just yet. And lie back down, you need more rest."

She looked pleadingly at the Director.

"I can't get you out of her without Doc's seal of approval, so my recommendation is that you stop trying to get me to overrule him on everything."

Wanting to argue that he'd been the one that had just gotten her unrestrained, she opened her mouth, but the Director cut her off as if he'd heard her thoughts.

"Surely you don't want to give him a reason to put those back on you."

Zoey groaned in frustration and flopped back down onto the bed, which was still fully reclined.

"Can I at least read through the reports we have so far from Tuesday so I can stay up to speed on things?"

"No, no, no. I want you to get some rest." Doctor Sanderson chimed in and looked pointedly at the Director, as if he were ordering him to leave.

"Don't agitate Doc, Zoey," the Director said as he left her once more. Once the room was quiet, it didn't take her long to fall asleep.

ZOEY

Zoey relished the feel of the scalding hot shower water cascading down on her. It was 10:45 on Saturday morning and Doctor Sanderson, after a significant amount of fussing at her to take things slow, had finally let her leave medtech and return to her cabin. The Director had her room AI deliver a message that they would begin Trevor's interrogation at 1400, and that she would need to make sure she ate lunch before joining him in his office to go over their action plan.

For the first time in days, her head felt clear enough for her to process Tuesday morning's events. Something about the substance the Maxwells' associate had put on her was bothering her. She tried to pick apart the feeling it gave her from the overall exhaustion she'd felt even before arriving at the bank that morning. Something seemed...familiar about it. Suddenly, it hit her like a stack of bricks, and she jumped out of the shower, splashing water all over her bathroom floor. She rushed to get dressed as quickly as possible and ran from her cabin, hair still dripping wet.

She ran through the maze of corridors as quickly as she could, slowing down only to sneak past medtech for fear of Doctor Sanderson catching her running. As soon as she was convinced she was in the clear, she took off running again. When she reached the wing that housed the conference rooms, she rounded a corner and ran full speed into the Director, knocking him down and causing him to drop the paperwork he'd been carrying. Zoey was thrown backwards herself by the force and took a nasty bump on the head as a result.

Outraged, the Director opened his mouth as if he were about to scream at her, but Zoey didn't give him the chance.

"Trevor helped them make it! He's been testing it here; we might be able to find his notes!"

The Director stood and glowered at Zoey, who gulped and rose unsteadily to her feet. The ground was wet behind her from her hair.

"You have thirty seconds, Zoey, to explain this or so help me, I am going to lock you in containment for the remainder of your life."

She took a deep breath and proceeded.

"The drug they used on me at the bank. I've felt the effects of it before, but a much lower dosage. Remember the mission in Dubai? That's why I couldn't get out of the box, and it took me too long to react. I felt *off* at the time, but I just chalked it up to being stuck in that box for so long. I'm probably not the only agent he's tested it on, either. Surely a few others have reported similar feelings?"

The Director looked at her thoughtfully, rage still flowing behind his eyes, and walked into the conference room behind him. He pressed a button on the intercom and told the field coordinator to pull the field reports of five other agents and deliver them to him immediately. After receiving confirmation from the field coordinator, he turned his attention back to Zoey.

"You could have called me, rather than running recklessly through the hallways. What if you'd hurt someone?"

"I'm sorry, I just couldn't think straight once that came to me and I wanted to let you know. I guess...I guess I should go get lunch and rest for a while..."

"I'll tell you what, you can stay and help me look over these reports and we can go ahead and start planning out this interrogation, but if Doc finds out, you have to tell him you lied about lunch and rest."

"Wouldn't he expect you to punish me for lying to you? It doesn't seem fair for me to get in trouble for following your plan."

"So, if he doesn't find out, you get away with knocking me over just then."

"Fair enough." She said, ready to jump back into work mode.

DIRECTOR

It had been some time since things felt normal between him and Zoey. With her attitude getting increasingly out of line over the past few months leading to all they'd gone through recently, he was glad to be working side by side with her, digging through files and making notes of specific information they needed from Trevor. It almost felt like she was enjoying being an agent again, and he was glad. Her willingness to continue by his side made his job for the Board much easier.

Despite her quick thinking as they worked through every possible angle, he could tell her energy was already fading. *I should send her back to her cabin, but interrogation is scheduled to start soon.*

"Are you ready to head over to the interrogation wing?"

She nodded at him.

"How much time will you give him to talk before we start using our...other methods?"

For the first time, the Director noticed that Zoey seemed almost sad about Trevor's betrayal.

"I *will* find out everything after what he did to you."

"I'm not worried about that, I just..."

She's not sad about his betrayal. She's actually worried about hurting him. This can't be happening.

"Zoey, if you don't have the stomach for what we have to do here, you should return to your cabin or, better yet, go check in with Doctor Sanderson. You seem a little *weak*."

He meant that to hit as an insult rather than an observation of her current physical status, and it seemed to work. She bristled at the word and squared her shoulders.

"I can handle it. Sir."

"Then act like it. Let's go."

Being angry at her actually helped him, though. He could let that rage radiate from his body toward Trevor. Any advantage he had was worth it in the end. When they reached the interrogation observation room, he and Zoey could see Trevor sitting on the other side of the mirrored glass. He looked disheveled and as if he hadn't slept in days. He probably hadn't, given that the Director's orders had been to keep him in a brightly lit room with loud static noise playing until the interrogation could finally begin. He lifted open a box and removed an earpiece, placing it in his ear, then pointed at the microphone on the desk in front of him.

"If anything he says contradicts any information we've gathered or triggers anything in your memory, let me know."

"Yes, sir."

Good. She's gotten herself back in line.

He left her alone and walked through the hallway, pausing to crack his neck before entering the interrogation side.

"Hello, Trevor. We need to have a talk."

ZOEY

Zoey sat alone in a conference room, slouching in a chair and spinning idly as she waited for Doctor Sanderson's arrival. Her knuckles on both hands were cracked open, bruised and bloody. He would be furious for a number of reasons, of course, but for once, Zoey didn't really care.

Trevor had started out strong during the Director's questioning and, after about an hour, the Director was ready to call in the interrogation team. Zoey had asked him if she could try talking to him first though, which earned her an irritated lecture from the Director, who thought she wasn't up to the job anymore. She finally convinced him to let her try though.

When she'd entered the interrogation room, she slid the chair reserved for the questioner over, blocking the door to make it more difficult for anyone else to enter. Before the Director had been able to react, Zoey lashed out at Trevor in rage, punching him repeatedly and yelling at him for his part in her near capture. She pointed out he'd almost gotten her killed the first time he tested the drug on her as well, and then started punching even harder.

Finally, a team had been able to break into the room and drag her back to the observation room. The Director had smirked at her before telling her to sit with him and they watched together as the interrogation unit began extracting information from Trevor.

Within two hours, they'd gotten every bit of information they could out of Trevor. She'd been certain the Director would be furious with her for assault, but he didn't mention it to her again. The plan was to discuss that information in the conference room, but Zoey's hands kept looking worse, so he went to get Doctor Sanderson.

Doctor Sanderson entered the conference room first followed by the Director, who looked to be maintaining a safe distance from the aggrieved medical professional. One look at her hands had him chastising her for a solid thirty minutes while he cleaned out the wounds and bandaged her hands.

"Thank you." She smiled sweetly at him, hoping to calm him down some, but that backfired.

"You're *not* welcome. What is going on with you? Have you no regard for your own well-being? What part of 'take it easy for a few days' made you think you should get in a brawl?"

"To be fair, he was restrained so it wasn't *really* a brawl."

She swore she could see the Director trying to hide a laugh.

"This is not a game, young lady! You were physically attacked and drugged and-"

"And I'm tired of being the punching bag, Doctor Sanderson. I know you have your job to do, but I have mine. I'm not going to sit this out just because you want me to sleep more; I'm going to find the Maxwells and everyone helping them come after us and I'm going to *end* them. So, thanks for all your concern, but I've got work to do now."

Without speaking, Doctor Sanderson turned to the Director, apparently curious as to whether he would let her speak to him like that. She was pretty curious, too.

"You released Zoey from your care this morning, Doc. It's my decision whether to let her work now, and she seems to be doing just fine. I'll let you know if you're needed again."

With that, Doctor Sanderson huffed out of the room. Zoey bit her bottom lip to keep herself from grinning, just in case she was about to get an earful about being disrespectful. No such conversation came, though, the Director choosing instead to sit next to her and split the paperwork on the table between the two of them.

"Let's get started on reviewing everything one more time before I get the field coordinator in here to start planning our next operation."

Once again, they fell into a familiar rhythm of working together. Once they'd itemized every piece of information of note, the Director called in the field coordinator. Zoey was actually relieved at her dismissal, ready to return to her cabin. She'd never admit it but, physically, she was feeling significantly worse since she attacked Trevor. Rest sounded good to her, but not before one more shower to wash the blood, hers and Trevor's, off her body.

ZOEY

"He's lying to you, Zoey."

Zoey looked coldly at Trevor, who was huddled in his cell, tear stains on his face, which looked pretty rough thanks to Zoey's handiwork. It was Sunday morning, and she had been too antsy to stay in bed long, despite the weariness she'd felt a few hours before.

"I'm not interested in any more ridiculous stories, Trevor. I just came to see if you'd remembered anything else overnight. I'm sure the Director would look favorably on any additional information you might be able to give us."

She didn't worry about keeping her voice down. There were no cameras or recording devices in this part of headquarters by design. It was best if no one ever found out the kind of things that happened to the people who had the misfortune of winding up there.

"I'm not telling you a story, I promise. This is all a lie. Doesn't it feel strange to you? I mean, no one is even allowed to meet the Board."

"I met them."

He gasped in shock.

"What? When?"

"Monday night, before you helped the Maxwells try to kill me. They're just people, Trevor."

"It was a disguise; they aren't like us. The Director's not like us. Can't you tell from his demeanor? Doesn't something seem off about him?"

"He seems like he always has. I've been here for two decades, and you've been here what, five minutes? Nothing was *off* about anything until you changed things."

"Just do me a favor- just think about it. Think about every interaction with him. Think about the day you met him. Spend some time really thinking about it. Promise you'll at least do that."

"Why should I promise you anything?"

"Despite what you think, I am your friend."

"Friends don't drug each other." Annoyed at the turn the conversation had taken, she began to walk away.

"Please, Zoey. Please think about it."

She made her way to the dining hall for breakfast. The Director hadn't ordered it but had told her before she left for her cabin Saturday night that she should probably try to get back on Doctor Sanderson's good side, in case she needed his services again. And he was right, because she could definitely see him holding her hostage in medtech for weeks out of spite.

Upon arriving at the dining hall, she found Doctor Sanderson and the Director eating together, engrossed in what appeared to be a serious conversation.

At least this should mostly work out in my favor.

She grabbed a tray and filled it with a pile of food and went in search of an empty table. She was still just frustrated enough with her conversation with Trevor that she didn't want to get roped into a group of people having a good time. But before she could settle on a spot, Doctor Sanderson called her over to his and the Director's table.

Well, this should be an absolute blast.

"Join us, we have plenty of space." He said darkly, as if he were daring her to defy the request in front of the Director. She didn't even bother looking to her boss in hopes of a way out, but she couldn't quite manage to fight off a sigh of irritation as she dropped down into a seat at the circular table.

The two men returned to their conversation, something about an agent who had returned from a mission with several broken bones, while Zoey picked her way through as much of her breakfast as she could. Occasionally Doctor Sanderson would break away from the discussion to instruct her to eat more of specific items. When she couldn't force herself to indulge him any further, she took the tray back to the counter and headed out of the dining hall, ignoring the Director's stare.

Unwilling to let the doctor get his way entirely, she went to her cabin and changed into gym clothes. She managed to get in a solid hour-long workout before tiring out completely.

Back in her cabin, Trevor's words crept into her mind. No matter how hard she tried to push them away, she still heard him begging her to think about the first time she met the Director. She sat down on her bed with her sketchbook and began drawing. She wanted to replace the drawing the Director had taken anyway, and still wondered why he had chosen that one. There was no way she would accept that his reasoning had been even remotely sentimental. As she sketched away, she lost herself in the art, and finally fell asleep with the sketchbook still in her hands.

ZOEY

She waited for her parents to make it down the hallway of their crumbling apartment building before realizing they weren't going to notice they'd left her behind. They'd been fighting again, all morning. This time, they were angry about the idea of having to take her shopping for new shoes. Her teacher had sent a note home saying Zoey had been getting picked on because her sneakers were held together by duct tape. It was her fault, of course. She was always so rough when she played.

Stepping on her tiptoes, she grabbed the extra key off the top of the refrigerator and followed after them, locking the apartment up behind herself. If she'd had any idea it was the last time she would ever be inside it, she probably would have grabbed the stuffed duck her grandfather had given her before his passing.

It didn't take her too long to catch up to them, but she wished it had. They were still fighting, each telling the other that it was his or her turn to spend time with her next. Zoey never was sure what she had done to make them dislike her so much, but they did. Suddenly, she felt a breeze and when she let her eyes follow its direction, she saw something. A shadowy figure without any real shape. She stared at it a bit longer before deciding her mind was playing tricks on her and turned back toward her parents.

As they made their way through the crowded streets toward a small second-hand store, Zoey got separated from her mom and dad once more.

She looked around, attempting to regain her bearings, a man approached her. He told her she looked lost and that he would help her find her way. All she needed to do was go with him. He wasn't the first older man to try to take her off on his own, though. Zoey collected all the anger she felt towards her parents within her and stamped on his foot as hard as she possibly could before stomping the other direction, chasing after the voices of the uncaring adults.

Zoey then felt the strange breeze once more, followed by stronger and stronger currents. She could almost hear voices whispering to her but couldn't make out what they were saying. By the time she realized that she and her parents had wound up in an alley several blocks away from their intended destination, darkness settled over them and a storm began to pick up, drowning out the noise of the city.

The next thing she knew, she was sitting on the dirty ground and realizing that her parents had dumped her there. She was overwhelmed with fear and couldn't remember which way to go to get home. They must have done it on purpose to make sure they would never have to deal with her again.

Then a stranger spoke to her.

"Are you okay? Please, please let me help you, Zoey."

They were the kindest words she had ever heard. Choking back her sobs, she wrapped her arms around the man's neck and let him carry her away to safety.

DIRECTOR

He stared out his bedroom window, concerned that Zoey had dreamed about that day. Ever since he had taken her, the memory had bonded him. She had many nightmares about it when she was young, and it took an excessive amount of time to force the memories out of her brain. He typically tried his best not to think of it himself, either from his own viewpoint or from that of her parents. Occasionally he did, though, and knew he shouldn't be surprised if his reminiscent trip a few days before had triggered something in her mind.

As best as he could tell, Zoey hadn't yet managed to break through any of the barriers he had embedded in her mind. Still, he'd have to get back into her mind to make sure everything he'd done to it was still intact. He couldn't even really be sure when she had drawn that picture, after all, and he couldn't risk her subconscious pushing the truth through to her.

The Director poured himself a glass of water before going to his study to review the notes from Trevor's interrogation once more. He had already made his report to the Board but wanted to be absolutely certain he hadn't missed anything in all the commotion. In all honesty, he had replayed the video of Zoey's brutal attack of Trevor multiple times, fearing she may have slipped him a message of some kind. She hadn't, he knew. Her rage had been too palpable. A small part of him regretted doubting her, but that came with the job- especially after he'd failed with so many recruits before her.

After hours of reviewing the notes, he made the determination that he hadn't missed anything. With Zoey out of medtech and everything holding together in a steady calm for the time being, he decided to go out for another feeding. This time he went a few towns over to cause less suspicion in his own backyard. He also took his time with finding a good source, allowing himself to really enjoy the hunt. After claiming his victim, he returned to once again rest the human body he so often wore.

The next morning, he went into his office early, which wasn't out of the ordinary for him on Mondays. His assistant already had a cup of coffee on his desk. The Director settled in with the beverage and began reading the various reports gathered up for him each night.

Strange. Why did Zoey visit Trevor?

He called medtech to find out if either Trevor or Zoey had been treated for any new injuries but neither of them had.

There has to be a logical explanation. I can just ask her. No, I can't. I need to handle this as I would any other infraction.

Prepared to drag the answers out of her, he alerted the AI system to deliver a message to her room. When she woke up, she was to report directly

to him. No stops along the way. A few moments passed before the AI's voice played back in his office, letting him know that Zoey wasn't in her cabin.
"Find her and get her here. Now."

ZOEY

"You have to give me something useful or I can't justify coming to see you again."

"Why did you come see me today?"

She thought about that for a moment before responding.

"I wanted to give you another chance to help yourself."

"You thought about it, didn't you? You thought about it, and something feels off."

"No. I thought about it, and it feels like the Director saved me. Do you have anything else that might be useful?"

"You didn't think hard enough then."

She rolled her eyes and began to walk away.

"I don't have time for this."

"Zoey, wait. If I tell you something else, will you promise to keep trying? If you just focus, I promise you'll see that I'm not wrong."

"Depends on what it is you can tell me."

"He's going to offer you a promotion soon. You can't take it. You'll never be able to get free."

"Your insider information is that I'm doing my job well?" She raised her eyebrow at him, looking at her watch as if she were well and truly bored with the conversation.

"Look, just promise you'll keep thinking it over and you won't rush to a decision on the promotion. Promise me that and I'll give you something to take back to him."

Normally, she wouldn't waste her time. But she was still so stunned by the knowledge that he had been working with the Maxwells that she was doing everything in her power to wrap her head around it.

"Fine. Start talking."

"The Maxwells aren't running a mom-and-pop operation. They've got big money backing them, and they answer to a group of people. Not quite like the Board, but there are other people in play. Which means, they are well connected. I don't know what their next plans are, Zoey, but I know they will eventually come back for the Director. They will try to bait both of you, because as long as your loyalties are here, you are a threat to them. They will go after someone you would both fight for and draw you out of DNP's safety. Whether you decide to stay with DNP or go with them, just be careful and take care of yourself."

She couldn't help but let a laugh escape.

"They'll try to come after us? Really, is that the best you have? Of course they will, Trevor. Jemma told me that much herself. If that's the best you can do then I am *definitely* wasting my time."

"Fine. They are going to try to take Doctor Sanderson."

"You're positive?"

"Yes."

"When?"

"They know his schedule pretty well by now. My guess is they'll grab him when he's on his way back for his next weeklong shift."

Next Monday. We can't risk them moving up their timeline and grabbing him now, so we'll have to go get him right away.

"Thank you, Trevor."

"You should let them take him. They'll take far better care of him."

"You mean like they took such good care of you?"

"None of them ever tried to punch me to death."

"How many of them did you help drug?"

When he didn't respond, she left the holding area. As soon as she rounded into the main building, an AI pad on the wall lit up, telling her that the Director was looking for her and that she should go to his office immediately.

Before breakfast means he's mad at me again. What did I do this time?

DIRECTOR

"You look tired. When I get to the vitals report, am I going to learn that you stayed up all night again?"

"No, sir. I slept; I just had some weird dreams."

He hadn't expected her to be up front about the dreams after all he'd put her through to get rid of them initially, but he was glad she did. It showed she was finally handing herself over to him fully. It also meant he wouldn't have to fight to drag that bit of information out of her, though he suspected the Trevor situation would play out differently.

One victory at a time.

"How were your dreams weird, Zoey?" He pointed her to the guest chair in his office once again and noticed a look of pure resignation on her face before she spoke.

"I guess it wasn't weird. I just haven't dreamed about that day in a long time and it kind of threw me for a loop."

"You're talking about the day I found you, I presume?"

"Yes, sir."

"Was there anything different about it this time?"

"No, sir. Still the same. My parents were fighting, I followed them, some guy tried to talk to me, then a storm came through and they left me in an alley I didn't recognize. And then you found me."

Well, that's a relief. I don't have time to tear through her mind again.

"Is this going to be a problem?"

"No, sir. I don't think so. I'm sure it was probably tied to everything that went on last week."

"If it happens again, I want you to let me know right away." This time he saw a flicker of fear in her eyes.

"Yes, sir."

"That's not why I told you to come here."

Zoey sat forward slightly in her seat but didn't say anything. Clearly, she was going to let him lead the conversation, which made him question how much she might actually still be hiding from him.

"Did you go see Trevor yesterday?"

A sigh of relief escaped his top agent as she settled back comfortably in the chair.

"I did. This morning, too."

His eyes flashed at that news.

"Zoey, I can't have you feeling sympathetic for our enemies and-"

"No sir, that's not what happened. Something's felt off since his interrogation. It all happened too quickly. I went back yesterday to try to get more out of him, but he kept saying he didn't have anything else. This morning, I remembered that he told me something yesterday about them trying to draw us out of headquarters. I had originally dismissed it because it doesn't exactly take an insider to know the Maxwells aren't done with whatever plans they have.

But anyway, I started thinking maybe I had cut him off before he could tell me any details about that plan. So, I went back this morning and found out they are planning to grab Doctor Sanderson. I was heading toward your office to tell you when I got the message that you wanted me here anyway."

He studied her closely, determining that she really was firmly on his side. Now was the time.

"I'll send a team out to pick up Doctor Sanderson."

"Can I go?"

"No, I need you here for something else."

"Okay."

He knew she was confused but appreciated the way she patiently waited while he made a call on his office line. He was calling the Board, but he didn't want Zoey to know that quite yet, so he didn't use the speakerphone.

"It's time."

Not even a full beat after he spoke the words, a voice responded telling him they were waiting for him. He hung up and looked at Zoey once more.

"We have another meeting with the Board today, Zoey. Would you like time to change or will you be wearing that?"

She looked down at her purple leggings and black t-shirt.

"I'll go change."

"No need to be overly formal, though. They want to see the real Zoey."

"Yes, sir."

He dismissed her then made a call to the field coordinator, giving instructions to prepare a team and send them to bring Doctor Sanderson back to headquarters. He wanted him safely on campus by the time he returned from his meeting.

ZOEY

If they want to get to know the real me, then that's what they are going to get.

Zoey stood in front of her full-length mirror, appraising her appearance. She still looked a little too thin, but some of the frailty had worn off. Her white hair fell in loose waves down just past her shoulders, and she wore smokey eyeshadow with a dark pink gloss. For clothing, she paired a long-sleeved black top that exposed a small portion of her midriff and black leather pants with a pair of flat black boots. They were her favorite boots for missions because she could move quickly and quietly in them.

She wasn't really sure what impression she was trying to give them. She was a fighter, she was strong, and she wasn't much for dresses and frills, despite how much time she'd spent in those at Mirror Bank. More than anything, she really just wanted to feel like herself again, and this look did the trick.

Pausing briefly to decide if anything about the look might anger the Director, she reminded herself that he was the one who told her not to bother with being so formal. Hopefully she didn't make him regret that decision. Zoey went to flip off the lights in her cabin, but her dream crashed over her.

What if you never get to come back?

It was a silly thought, of course. She was just going for a meeting with the Board. Still, she couldn't fight the nagging sensation that something was off and grabbed her favorite switchblade from a box in her closet before locking up and making her way to the vehicle bay, stopping only to tell an AI panel on the wall to let the Director know she would be waiting at the cars. He probably would be agitated that she hadn't come to him first, but she was too focused on trying to figure out why the Board might want to see her again to think about that.

When she got to the line of SUVS and spotted the Director's specific one, she leaned against a concrete column nearby and waited. Voices carried her way, and she noticed the Director's driver running to the car, with several members of the security team loading up in similar vehicles. She wondered whether she would be in one of those or if the Director would demand she ride with him once again.

Zoey didn't have to wait long for her answer though, as the Director came out of headquarters shortly after the others. His eyes found her immediately, and he looked almost shocked, but almost immediately returned to his typical poker face.

"All of the options you had, and this is what you chose?"

"You told me they wanted to meet the real me."

"I would say I was surprised that this felt like the real you, but I'm not."

"You looked a tiny bit surprised."

"Not because you feel like this...'look' explains who you are, but because you've chosen to commit that much to it given the meeting we are about to have." He beckoned her to join him in his vehicle, and she did without hesitation.

"What meeting are we about to have?" She couldn't help it. She was dying to know why she was getting to see the Board again for a second time, especially when the Director hadn't given her any indication that she was in trouble for anything.

"I'm presenting my formal recommendation that you begin training as a Director."

"You're doing what?"

She could barely think as the vehicles began rolling out of the garage.

"Put your seatbelt on, Zoey."

She obediently fastened her belt, but never took her eyes off the Director, searching for any hint that he was joking.

"You've worked very hard for a long time, and this past week has really pushed you. Yet your loyalties never wavered. I think you've earned the chance to move up within the organization."

'He's going to offer you a promotion soon.'

"Do you think that's a good idea?"

"Look Zoey, if you're going to be ungrateful or refuse, let me know now before I let myself look like an idiot in front of the Board. I thought you might welcome the chance to expand outside of our specific headquarters, but if you prefer to just keep working assignments for the rest of your life we can turn around and go back to headquarters."

"No, sir! I mean, I'm honored, I am. I am just really surprised. Thank you, it really does mean a lot that you would want to promote me."

It did. Trevor wouldn't take this away from her, either. This was her chance to do more, to be in control of herself. She wouldn't let a traitor ruin that for her now that she finally had won over the Director. Zoey flashed a big smile at him and settled back into her seat, trying her best not to fidget from the nerves or excitement over what was about to happen.

ZOEY

Are you okay? Please, please let me help you, Zoey.

The phrase kept repeating through her mind, but she had no idea why. Maybe it was just because she'd thought about that night several times recently. She was also feeling pretty tired and weak at the moment, so she wasn't able to process things very clearly.

Trying to force the thoughts out of her mind, she shifted her focus back to the Director's declaration that she was ready to start training for her promotion. Honestly, she never thought the day would come and, now that it had, her mind was reeling.

He's going to offer you a promotion soon. You can't take it. You'll never be able to get free.

Whatever, Trevor. You're not going to ruin my moment just because you were stupid enough to betray us.

"I thought you'd be happier about this."

Zoey turned her attention to the Director, who was eyeing her intently.

"I am happy. Very! I think I'm just a little nervous." She lit up inside at the smile he gave her in response.

"It's not very often that you get nervous. I'm glad to know you plan to accept."

"I couldn't imagine even considering turning it down!"

Something about his continued smile threw her off, making him appear almost satisfied about something. She chose not to dwell on that, though, as she was sure he was probably just happy that she'd finally stepped up to show her true potential.

Eventually she realized she was fidgeting with anticipatory energy and quickly made herself stop, but the Director just let out a low chuckle.

"It's okay, Zoey. You won't get in trouble for being excited about this amazing opportunity.'

She flashed a grin at him, then continued staring out the window as they made their way through the mostly empty city streets toward the Boardroom.

Are you okay? Please, please let me help you, Zoey.

DIRECTOR

Never one to brag, the Director had to admit that he was quite proud of himself. Finally, he would present a recruit to the Board. She would begin her real training and would eventually be granted the Knight Mare title herself. They would be unstoppable together.

The Director couldn't help but watch Zoey as she moved continuously in her seat and a part of him wondered if she was regretting her wardrobe choice. When he told her the Board wanted to see the real her, there was a part of him that meant he'd like to see that as well. Never would he have selected that specific look for her, but she wore it well. Her confidence in it was a good distraction from her overall physical frailty. He'd have to fix that, of course. The Board would need her in her best condition before they could begin her transformation. He even considered having the interrogation chip removed, but he would wait on that until he knew things were going smoothly in her training.

He looked out his own window, noting the barren streets. He'd seen this before, when he'd been promoted. The Board had a tendency to push a lot of energy during these events that most people recoiled from, so the city had been largely shut down. Even the news stations were reporting that the police had urged everyone to stay home, citing potential threats they had not been able to fully investigate yet. A couple stragglers lingered, but all businesses were closed. He knew by the time they left the Boardroom, no one would be around.

Rather than dropping them off at the street entrance, the three SUVs circled behind the building and parked in a garage. Given the event set to occur and the fact that the Maxwells were a budding threat, the security team refused to allow the Director to spend much, if any, time in the open air. He didn't enjoy that, but he had long ago learned it was part of the job. Pausing for a moment before exiting the car, he wondered how Zoey would handle herself in the same situation. She would have to find some way to understand that the Board would not allow her to risk her safety once she became transformed. A member of the team opened his door and he slid out of the vehicle, walking to the other side to meet Zoey. He gave her a look which he hoped conveyed how serious this matter would be.

"Are you ready?"

"Yes, sir."

We are off to a good start, then.

"Let's go inside."

And he walked forward, following only two security members while the remainder waited in the garage until orders were given that it was time to leave after the promotion. Once they reached the stairwell, the two guards led them up a poorly lit but clean set of stairs that escorted them to the Boardroom's main lobby. Once safely inside the lobby, they returned downstairs to keep watch with the others. After he was sure they'd gone he turned to speak at Zoey, but she was no longer beside him. Instead, he found her across the room, sitting on the bench where he'd left her the first time he ever brought her to the Boardroom, kicking her feet out in front of her as if she were just a child once more.

ZOEY

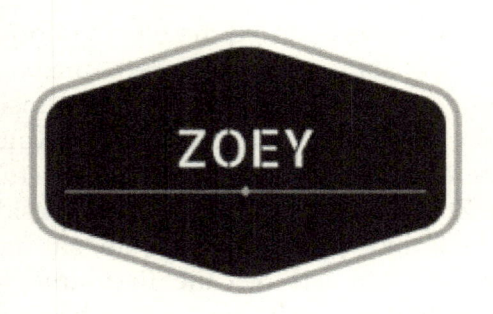

She held her legs in the air, gently kicking her feet up and down without realizing she was doing it. Suddenly she realized that she'd done this very thing before, as she could almost see her nine-year-old self sitting next to her. The sensation was strange especially considering that Zoey had not remembered this part of that evening before now. Previously, she had only remembered that the Director saved her in the alley, that he'd brought her to the Boardroom, and that she'd sat waiting for him before he took her to headquarters. She hadn't remembered anything specifically about what she'd done while she was waiting.

Are you okay? Please, please let me help you, Zoey.

Noticing the Director walking toward her, she spoke up so he could hear her well.

"Did I really tell you that this place was boring when I was a kid?" Zoey was shocked at her own question, not sure where that memory came from either.

The Director studied her, looking slightly concerned. *No, he just wants to make sure I don't say or do something stupid that will get him in trouble with the Board.*

"You did. And I believe I told you to sit still and not speak unless spoken to first." Without a moment's hesitation she placed her feet flat on the ground, feeling like an errant child once more. Neither of them spoke again as they waited, Zoey still seated w while the Director stood next to her, his hands in his pockets.

He has the remote for the interrogation chip. Am I not really getting promoted? Should I have worn a suit?

Though she sat still anticipating a surge of pain, none came, and she allowed herself to relax once more.

He always has it with him; he's just standing there right now. No big deal.

The heavy doors to the Boardroom opened silently. It was time. Zoey stood and walked through with the Director who clearly didn't feel the need to steer her in the correct direction again. Standing shoulder to shoulder, they waited another thirty minutes or so before the Board members finally made their appearance. Somewhat of an appearance, Zoey realized, as they kept themselves largely hidden in the shadows. She wasn't able to make out their faces this time, or any distinguishing characteristics for that matter.

The Shadow Dynasty. It kinda fits.

A voice spoke, but Zoey couldn't find its source. Rather, it sounded like the voice had been projected around the entire room, as if all the members were speaking at once, despite it being singular in nature.

"Director, we understand you are prepared to make a presentation to the Board?"

"I am."

She noted that he did not speak loudly at all, but the Board seemed to hear him just fine anyway. For a quick second, she allowed herself to look at him and was thrown off by his dark expression.

Are you okay? Please, please let me help you, Zoey.

A shiver ran down her spine and she looked forward once more, determined to keep her intrusive thoughts from ruining her big, albeit weird, moment.

"You may proceed."

The Director took a small step forward, his hands no longer in his pockets.

"Based on exemplary service and a showing of unyielding loyalty, it is my recommendation at this time that Zoey Parks be promoted and begin training to become a full Director for this Board, effective immediately."

A chill rushed through the air in the room.

"Zoey Parks, are you willing to begin Directorship training and accept additional responsibility on behalf of the Board?"

This is way weirder than I thought it would be.

"Yes, sir. Ma'am. I'm sorry. I'm not sure who I'm answering."

The Director looked back at her incredulously and she hastened to correct her response.

"Yes, I am."

"Then it is time for the initiation procedure to begin. Zoey, please kneel before the Board."

Hang on. Kneel? What? Why would I-

"The Board told you to kneel Zoey, so *kneel*."

His voice was so different. He sounded almost like the Board member had, as if his voice had been projected all around her. She could feel winds gathering up around her despite the fact that they were indoors.

Something doesn't feel right.

She didn't have much time to think though as a gust pushed her forward, as if it were trying to force her to obey the command. Remembering that the Director was all too willing to hurt her for failing to follow orders, she allowed her body to move with the air that was pushing her and kneeled, her left knee on the ground and her arm resting on her right.

Are you okay? Please, please let me help you, Zoey. Something's wrong.

"Zoey Parks, you have been selected to begin training for promotion to a Director of one of our many DNP branches. As part of this service, we will require your mind, body, soul- your whole being as an offering to us."

Are you okay? Please, please let me help you, Zoey.

"Pledge your allegiance now to the Board so that your training may begin."

But she couldn't speak. All she could think about were those first words the Director ever spoke to her. Then his voice tore through her mind.

"Zoey, do not make me regret this choice." He was growling at her, and she could feel the anger rushing from him.

Are you okay? Please, please let me help you, Zoey.

"I never said my name." She whispered so low that no one could make out what she'd said.

"Speak up." His voice commanded.

In one quick movement, Zoey pulled the knife from her right boot and swept the Director's legs out from under him with her left leg. Without giving him time to react, she pounced on top of him, holding the knife to his throat.

"I said I never told you my name. When we met you asked me to let you help me, and you called me Zoey. But I didn't say anything to you before you spoke. So, you had no way of knowing my name."

Agony coursed through her, causing her to lose her grip on the knife. The Director attempted to stand but Zoey kicked him while flailing and screaming, causing him to fall back once more. Unable to withstand much more, she allowed the heel of her left foot to crash down on the Director's hand, causing him to drop the device's remote. Zoey grabbed it and pressed it repeatedly until the pain ceased. She could feel a flurry of movement behind her, and she ran, refusing to look back. All she knew was she had to get away quickly.

Running as hard as she could, she made it out of the building only to realize there were no crowds of people for her to blend into as she escaped. Zoey turned to look back at the Boardroom and saw the Director exiting the building at a leisurely pace. She rounded the first corner she could and pressed on, her heart pounding in her chest. Her weakness was already weighing her down, making it hard to breathe as she sprinted. A cloud of smoky tendrils appeared in front of her, and she stopped in her tracks. They held her mesmerized for a moment before they advanced on her. She had to stifle a scream of fear then turned to run in the other direction as they chased her. Every time she made progress in her getaway, they reappeared before her, pushing her to choose another path. Doing her best to ignore the residual pain from the interrogation device and the fact that she felt like her lungs were about to explode, she continued racing away from the tendrils each time they appeared. When she finally couldn't run any longer, she dropped to her knees beside a dumpster where she began dry heaving from the stress on her fragile body.

A horrific sensation filled her, and she looked up to realize she was in *that* alley. The smoky tendrils reappeared, and she stood shakily, backing into the alley with nowhere else to go. A burst of darker smoke appeared within them for a moment and then the Director stepped through as if he'd simply walked through a curtain. She frantically looked around for a way to escape but found nothing.

"Give me the remote, Zoey."

He was calm and commanding. As terrified as she was, she was able to think clearly enough to know if she handed it over, things would get much worse.

"No."

"I believe you meant no, sir, but that's still a problematic answer for me."

He advanced on her, and she took another step back, finding her back literally against the wall behind her.

DIRECTOR

"Give it to me."

None of them had accounted for her memories to start returning and, even if they had, no one considered that phrase a danger when altering her mind initially. For now, the Board was angrier at her than him, so he had a small window of opportunity to get things back under his control. Zoey didn't budge at his second demand for the device, and he sighed deeply.

"This is one of those times you will regret not doing as you're told."

"Of all the regrets I have right now, not letting you torture me is pretty low on the list."

"Twenty-one years ago, I swore to the Board that I would stamp that infernal attitude out of you and, tonight, I'm going to let myself enjoy that process."

He held his right hand up and the Whispers drew in circling around it. The Director relished the feel of their kinetic energy for a few moments, allowing Zoey's anticipation to grow. Without warning, he flicked his hand and the Whispers rushed toward her, obeying his silent command to retrieve the remote. They split into two groups and wrapped themselves tightly against each of Zoey's wrist. He watched as she tried desperately to fight away from them before the Whispers around her right wrist pulled her arm straight up in the air, bending it behind her back and holding her in place, so that her right elbow was next to her ear, pointed toward the sky. Her left wrist remained at her side, the Whispers dancing around it.

"Now will you hand over the control?"

"You'll have to try to pry it from my grip." She spoke through gritted teeth, obviously feeling the pain in her right arm from the uncomfortable pull.

"Perhaps that's another phrase you should add to your list of regrets." He twisted his own arm slightly and the Whispers around her left wrist tightened, wrenching it in two different directions at once. He heard the bones snap before she cried out in pain and the remote clattered to the ground. With another swift motion he ordered the Whispers to restrain her left arm the same way they did the right and she fell to her knees from the pressure on her broken wrist. He called another group of Whispers, and they retrieved the remote, depositing it within his hand. He then had the third group form a wall blocking the alley off from the street. No one would see them; no one would hear them. As they formed their barricade, he could see realization dawn on Zoey's face, and she struggled uselessly against her bonds in an attempt to get away.

"Apologize for your behavior." He spat the words at her all while knowing she would not do as he requested. Tears still streaming down her face, she spit at him, managing to catch one of his shoes.

"You must have misunderstood me. Let me help you try to understand." Glaring at her, he pressed the button and moved the switch on the side to maximum level. Zoey convulsed as she shrieked in anguish, unable to fall to the ground as the Whispers kept her locked in place.

The Director allowed it to continue a bit longer before turning off the device. He knelt down in front of Zoey and cupped her chin in his hand, forcing her head up to look him in the eyes.

"Please, please let me help you, Zoey." He mocked her before he shoved her face away and started the device again, watching her fight for her freedom in an attempt to stop the pain. He commanded the Whispers to pull tighter and the bones in her left wrist cracked more.

"Apologize." He used his power to project his voice ensuring that she would hear him over her wails.

"I'm. I'm. S-s-s-sorry. I'm sor. Sorry." He allowed the pain to continue while watching her twist and turn, unable to find relief. Finally, he showed her mercy, even allowing the Whispers to release her. Zoey cried out once more as she fell forward onto the ground, the weight mangling her wrist further.

She curled into a ball, broken from the torture. He could have ended it and taken control of her mind then, but he wanted to make sure she never forgot this moment. So, he stood over her waiting for her to catch her breath before kicking her hard in the ribs, knocking her over onto her back. The Director leaned down and grabbed her by the throat, calling on the Whispers both to help him tighten his grip and to keep Zoey from trying to fight away.

"I'm going to enter your mind, Zoey, and I'm going to take it over. You will remember this moment, the pain you've felt in this alley. It will be a reminder of what defiance earns you. But when I'm finished in that head of yours, you will have no choice but to do as you're told. You will follow orders without question, not that you'd even be able to question them. You will surrender to the Shadow Dynasty, and you'll join me as a Knight Mare. You will never again act, speak, or think without my express permission."

Her eyes were wide with terror as he transformed and pushed himself into her body, settling into her brain.

ZOEY

Zoey awoke in a familiar room, but she couldn't place why. A man and woman bustled about, whispering to each other. She started to sit up to figure out what was happening, but a male voice to her right stopped her.

"Don't get up unless you get permission from Doctor Sanderson or me."

She looked toward the voice and saw the Director.

"Yes, sir." She laid back down.

My voice sounds strange.

Doctor Sanderson, the man she had noticed first, approached her gazing at her left side. She looked down to see her left arm tightly wrapped in a thick brace.

"Don't mess with that, either."

The Director was pointing at her wrist.

Why am I here? I don't want to be here. I don't want to be anywhere near him.

"Yes, sir."

Why do I keep saying that? I don't trust him.

Doctor Sanderson interrupted her thoughts.

"Why on earth would you go jump in front of a moving vehicle, Zoey? You're lucky to be alive."

"The driver tried to hit the Director." Her tone was flat.

No! That's not what happened! Why can't I tell him how dangerous the Director is?

Because I won't let you.

Zoey whipped her head toward the Director. She'd heard his voice, but in her head.

But how? No this doesn't make sense.

Let it go, Zoey. Pay attention to Doc.

Her body obeyed immediately, her eyes locking onto the physician, fear gripping her as she realized the Director was somehow controlling her every move, prying into her every thought. She couldn't even open her mouth to speak without him releasing the power he had over her to allow it. So instead of screaming all the things she desperately wanted Doctor Sanderson to know, she sat there patiently with a vacant expression. When the doctor finally declared that he didn't believe Zoey had a concussion, the Director spoke once more.

"Doc, could Zoey and I have a moment to discuss a few things?"

When the doctor looked at Zoey and found only a blank face, he responded.

"Sure, sure. I need to track down the results from the x-rays on her ribs anyway."

Once he knew they had their privacy, the Director commanded Zoey to look at him once more, which she did immediately.

"Do you not remember our chat in the alley, Zoey?" He immediately flooded her mind with memories of her running away and all the pain he caused her. The influx ended with the memory of him telling her that he would take over her mind and she would be powerless to do anything outside of what he desired.

Stop. Stop, please. I'll do anything, just stop this.

But I can already assure that you'll do anything you're told, and this makes my life much easier.

Let me go.

"I'll never let you go, Zoey. You belong to us now, to the Shadow Dynasty. We won't free you from that."

I'll find a way out.

The Director reached into his jacket pocket and produced Zoey's knife-the one she'd held at his throat in the Boardroom.

Take it, Zoey.

Her right-hand shaking, she reached forward and took hold of the knife. And then, the next thing she knew, she was holding it up to her own throat, pressing it firmly into her skin.

"Do you really believe you can stop this? Do you truly think that you can overpower me now?"

The blade pushed harder inward, but Zoey was helpless to stop it. Fortunately, the sound of footsteps approaching interrupted the Director's show of power and he took the knife back from her, concealing it from Doctor Sanderson's view.

"She's got a set of small fractures in her ribs. I want to bandage them up and keep her here tonight."

"Does she need to stay, or are you just being overly protective?"

"Director, with a broken wrist and some broken ribs, she needs to remain as inactive as possible. It really would be best for her to stay here."

"You can bandage her up and keep her for a couple hours, but then I want her back in her cabin. We have an early day tomorrow."

"Sir-"

"Doctor Sanderson, need I remind you that ultimately you answer to me?"

"No, sir. I'm sure...I'm sure she'll be fine. I'll get her out of here once we're all finished."

"Thank you."

You may speak to Doctor Sanderson, but you will not tell him anything about what really happened.

Zoey watched as the Director exited and felt a small surge of relief as she realized she was able to speak on her own accord. She sat up so that the doctor could wrap up her side, then sat back as he declared he wanted to readjust her wrist brace to make sure everything was kept in place. Before starting, he wrote something on a notepad that Zoey couldn't see then set about freeing her left wrist.

"You know, Zoey, broken bones aren't always that bad. Surely you've been injured on missions and been able to turn that into an advantage by shifting all of your focus to the task at hand."

"Not really." She was surprised by how easy it was to speak. "It's actually kind of the opposite. I probably focus more on the pain."

"Why do you do that?"

"Because when I'm in pain, I can wear it like a mask, like I'm not strong enough to do what I need to do. When you let people think you are weak, you can surprise them with your strength."

"Interesting. . ."

Without warning, he pushed hard on her wrist, nearly causing her to vomit from the pain. While she was still in a state of shock and unbearable agony, he held up the notepad for her to read.

I'm working with Trevor. We will find a way to get him out of your head. Don't lose hope.

He squeezed on her arm once more and dropped the notepad, then began gently realigning it and tightening the brace back into place.

"Just focus on the pain, Zoey, and it will all be okay."

DIRECTOR

While inside her mind in the alley, the Director realized that Trevor was the initial trigger for Zoey's influx of memories which led to the almost catastrophic events at the Boardroom. She had certainly given too much time and consideration to his words. This revelation also told the Director that Trevor cared a great deal for Zoey, and he was ready to use that information to his benefit.

He stood outside his office, watching as she approached him almost robotically. It killed him that she no longer needed or even wanted him, but he didn't have time to play games with her anymore. The Board had expectations and he was going to meet them.

"I still don't believe Trevor has told us everything he knows, so we are going to pay him another visit."

"Yes, sir." He could feel her trying to fight his influence and instantly commanded her to start walking towards the area where Trevor was still being held. Her movements were stiff, which annoyed him.

Stop trying to fight back or I'll make it worse. Besides, you look ridiculous.

Her body relaxed and she transitioned into a more natural gait.

We aren't the enemies, Zoey. I'm trying to help you. You just have to let me.

He knew the effect the words would have on her, given the first phrase he'd ever spoken to the girl, and he was right.

If this is helping, I don't want it.

If I hadn't helped you when you were a child, you'd be in a much worse situation.

Is it really helping if you caused the situation to begin with, though?

They didn't want you.

He felt her flinching within her mind, as if the words had almost caused her physical pain, and he allowed them to walk the rest of their path in silence. Trevor jumped up from his seated position on the floor when he saw them approaching his cell.

"I think you're still holding out on us, Trevor. Don't you, Zoey?"

"Yes, sir."

This was going to be fun.

"I'm not. I've told you everything. I warned you about Doctor Sanderson."

The Director used Zoey to respond on his behalf.

"You did. But Doctor Sanderson had already agreed to fill in this week for Doctor Morris and, it turns out, he was already gathering his things to return to headquarters when our team got to his home."

Trevor alternately eyed Zoey and the Director, apparently thrown off by her tone. The Director resumed the conversation.

"You had access to all schedules, so surely you already knew he'd planned to be here. Doctor Morris has been scheduled to be away for quite some time"

"I was just telling you what I heard from Jemma. That's all the information I had."

"You're lying." Zoey spoke, and the Director could again feel her frustration.

"I'm not. I swear."

"Zoey, why don't you take a step forward and ask Trevor one more time to tell us what he's withholding?"

She obeyed instantly, taking a step closer to the cell. While she repeated the request to Trevor, the Director fished the interrogation remote from his pocket. When Trevor didn't answer immediately, he pressed the button on it and released enough of his power over his captive agent to allow her to fall to the ground as he sent the pain coursing through her body. "Maybe it's coming back to you now?" The Director asked Trevor who paced frantically, completely unable to help the screaming girl. He still said nothing, though, and the Director forced Zoey to beg Trevor for the information. That seemed to break him down as he yelled for the Director to stop. He did, and regained control over her mind.

Stand up next to me and don't say a word.

She did, and Trevor looked positively frightened. The Director fought back a smile as he appreciated the way she stood, stone still, waiting for his next command.

"Unless you want to see that show again, I suggest you hurry up."

"They can contain the Whispers. Okay? They created a weapon that allows them to trap them and contain them so that none of you can control them anymore. They are testing the weapon, or they were. I don't know if they finished yet. But I hope I'm there when they come for you and take away your biggest source of power. I hope I'm there when you lose."

Zoey collapsed in affliction once more and the Director watched as Trevor screamed for someone to help, reaching desperately through the bars on his cell to try to save her. Once he'd been thoroughly entertained by the show, he released her once again.

Get up. Stand behind me and turn your back toward Trevor.

Without batting an eye, she did so, and the Director took a menacing step toward Trevor.

"You all can trap as many of the Whispers as you want. There are far too many for you to take them all. But, even if you did, I don't need the Whispers now. I have a much stronger weapon against you all. I have *Zoey*."

He stepped aside so that Trevor could see her back, then walked away. Once he'd gotten several paces, he spoke aloud.

"Come, Zoey."

"Yes, sir."

And she did, without even attempting to look back at Trevor.

TREVOR

"He's gotten into her mind."

Trevor slammed his hand against the wall of his cell in frustration.

"That's what he meant when he said he didn't need the Whispers anymore, and why she didn't fight him when they were here earlier. I've never seen her so deferential. He's torturing her, Doc. You've got to get her out of here."

"What? Torturing her how?"

Trevor recounted the events of the Director's latest interrogation and the doctor's face filled with fury.

"That's what she meant when I was removing the tracking device. She asked something about inventing similar technology for the interrogation simulator, but he warned her off. It didn't make sense, because it can be removed the same way, but I didn't know he had left one in her and was still using it."

"You've got to find a way to get it out of her then."

"That's easier said than done."

Trevor stared sadly at Doctor Sanderson before whispering.

"When did he do it, Doc? When did he take her mind?"

"Last night. He took her to the Board to present her for a promotion and when they returned, she had a broken wrist, some fractured ribs, and a nasty bump on her head. She said she jumped in front of a car to push the Director out of the way, but I could see in her eyes that he's taken over."

"Have you updated Jemma yet? Zoey's not safe, you've got to get her out of here."

"No, there's been no time. And I'm working on it. I can pass messages to her when she's in extreme pain because she's able to mask her thoughts when she's hurting. But I can't just walk out with her. The Director won't let her out of his sight for long and even if he did, he'd still be in her head. We can't move her until we figure out a way to get him out of there."

A brief pause fell over them as the sound of a clanking door came from down the hallway. Doctor Sanderson quickly gathered up his things and started to walk away.

"I can't stay here with you much longer. If you and I are going to continue meeting, you're going to need new injuries that need treating."

"What should I do, bash my head against the wall repeatedly?"

"Ironically, isn't that what you're doing already, stuck in there?"

JEMMA

Jemma and Todd were camped out on top of an unused building in a small town about seven hundred miles away. They believed they finally had all the technology in place to capture Whispers, and the small sphere had withstood several testing rounds. Now, they were going to go up against a Knight Mare to see if it would work in a real-life situation.

While Todd was antsy to get the mission started, Jemma was distracted. Doctor Sanderson and Trevor had put everything on the line to help their cause. Now, Trevor was locked away and Doctor Sanderson could barely communicate for fear of getting caught. He'd told her just a few minutes before she and Todd set out to trail the Knight Mare that the Director had forcibly taken Zoey. She was shocked. Knight Mares always lured their prey in, leading them to want the change. Jemma had never heard of one so brazenly forcing a recruit into service to the Shadow Dynasty. She'd made Todd promise her that, if this new weapon worked, they would focus all of their energy on taking down the Director and rescuing their friends and finding a way to save

Zoey. Todd had argued with Jemma about that last part. He told her that Zoey had been given a way out and she chose to stay, so what was happening to her was her own fault. But Jemma couldn't accept that. She saw Zoey's loyalty to the Director for what it was- a fear of losing the one constant she'd ever had in her life. And he'd repaid her by stealing the very essence of who she was. Jemma would work with Doctor Sanderson to do whatever she could to release Zoey from the Director's clutches. In the meantime, she requested that the doctor remove the interrogation device as soon as he could reasonably find a way to do so.

Todd reached over and took her hand, which gave her some comfort as they waited impatiently. Finally, after they'd spent about an hour in the humid outdoors, the target they'd determined was a Knight Mare emerged in human form. On cue, a couple agents who'd volunteered to be bait began arguing. Their voices carried to the woman, and she turned toward them. Jemma waited with building anticipation until she'd stepped around the corner and Todd at long last engaged the sphere hidden behind some trash. A bright light erupted, and a whirl of Whispers began peeling off the woman, hurtling into the light. She cried out in rage as the entire pack was devoured by the sphere. One of the arguing agents knocked her down, grabbed the sphere, and ran to a waiting vehicle while Jemma and Todd quietly raced back inside the building and waited for the Knight Mare to leave.

When they all met up at the rendezvous spot, the agent held the sphere out to Jemma, a smile lighting his face. Jemma looked at the sphere in wonder, taking in the sight of the Whispers tumbling around in a bright white space. She turned to Todd and gave him a small kiss.

"We can do it. We can start fighting back."

DIRECTOR

The Director found himself frustrated with the time it was taking for Zoey's wrist to heal. While he had commanded the Whispers to break it, he hadn't intended for them to cause quite such excessive damage. When he used the interrogation device against her, he could plan to block himself from her reaction, but the random spikes in pain coming from her wrist were unexpected and intrusive. It occurred to him that he likely wouldn't even have cared about that if he hadn't gotten flashes of white-hot pain from the connection in her mind. He made a mental note to ask Doctor Sanderson about surgically repairing it and possibly giving her painkillers. Typically, that was a no-go for all agents, but he'd found himself willing to make the exception for his own comfort.

News had reached him early that morning that a team had successfully stolen another Knight Mare's Whispers. He'd alerted the Board to the information he extracted from Trevor, but the message didn't get out quickly enough to everyone. The Board announced that they had "handled" the affected Knight Mare, and he shuddered to think what that meant. The Board tasked him with using all available resources to stop the Maxwells and he was reading through his copious notes on the couple when another flash of Zoey's pain blindsided him.

Come to my office immediately.

He supposed he should have been grateful that she wasn't constantly complaining about it, but the truth was he could have ignored that much easier than the random bursts of torturous agony. The Director was in the middle of refocusing his thoughts on the task in front of him when Zoey arrived. She stood silently, awaiting his next command. When he finally looked up at her, he noticed her eyes were red as if she'd been crying. He hadn't felt that himself, but he supposed it was likely due to the overwhelming sensation of pain.

"Is it your wrist?"

"Yes, sir."

"Are you removing the brace?"

"No, sir."

"We have a lot of work to do if we are going to track down the Maxwells and I can't keep being distracted like this. Learn to deal with it in a less intrusive way until I can talk to Doctor Sanderson about other options."

"Yes, sir."

I'm trying to deal with it.

Try harder.

"Yes, sir."

"Good. Here's the location where the Maxwells made their attack last night." he handed her a map printout. "Go get set up in the conference room with a list of potential hideouts near that spot and I'll be there soon. We need to try to flush them out quickly."

Fury filled him as he felt her try to fight the command.

"Go now or I'll break the other wrist too."

"Yes, sir."

He watched her exit, then threw his pen on the desk and sat back in his chair. Despite everything, he had to admit that she was still impressively strong-willed.

She'll make an excellent servant to the Dynasty once she finally surrenders.

TREVOR

"So, it really worked?"

Trevor asked Doctor Sanderson, buzzing with excited energy while the doctor stitched a cut on his forehead. When his most recent meal had been brought to him, he pretended to be weak and faked passing out, intending for that alone to be enough for them to call Doctor Sanderson. But he hadn't accounted for *where* he was falling and managed to hit his forehead squarely on one of the metal bars keeping him confined.

At least he'll have to come check for infections and stuff.

"Yes. I haven't received details from them, but Zoey managed to get a note to me. The Director is most upset about it."

"How did she get you a note without the Director seeing what she wrote?"

"I told you before I could pass messages to her by hiding them behind pain. She's been hurting herself when she needs to get a message to me. Apparently, the pain affects him too, so I think a part of her has enjoyed that."

"You know how ridiculous that sounds right? She can only find happiness if she hurts herself. She needs our help, Doc."

"And I suppose you've come up with a plan to get out of this cell, kick the Director out of her mind, and get the three of us away from here without being caught?"

"It doesn't feel like you're doing much planning either."

Trevor was furious that Doctor Sanderson had accused him of doing nothing. It wasn't his fault he was in the cell in the first place. Jemma should have never told Zoey he was involved. He didn't know that he'd ever be able to forgive her for that slip in judgment.

"We have to do this carefully, Trevor. Right now, we know that Zoey is still in there. He hasn't imposed on her enough to break her completely. She's not a Knight Mare yet. The things he sees as Zoey's faults are her greatest weapons against him. She will not allow herself to be fully taken by the Director."

"I hope you're right. Because if he finds out about your covert conversations, he'll kill all three of us before we ever get a chance to get out of here."

"I am right. Trust me. Zoey has information on where Jemma and Todd were last, and we are working out a way to keep the Director from closing in on them. In the meantime, I'm set to have a call from someone on their team tonight and I can finally fill them in on what all has been going on here. Just stay with me, Trevor. We're going to find a way out."

"I want to be there the day Zoey kills the Director."

"We all do."

Doctor Sanderson finished stitching Trevor's head.

"I know we talked about banging your head against the wall, but let's try to avoid any more head trauma in the future. You don't want to cause permanent damage."

"Yeah, thanks. I'll keep that in mind."

"I will do everything I can to get you out of here, you know that, right?"

Trevor sighed.

"I'm not the priority. If Zoey can really withstand the force of a Knight Mare in her head, all of our attention has to be focused on her. Even if we can stop the Whispers, the Knight Mare's still have powers we can't combat. Zoey might be our only chance of winning this war."

"I'm still going to try to save you, too."

"I know."

As Doctor Sanderson walked away Trevor reflected on the conversation, rolling the small scalpel he'd stolen from the doctor's bag in his fingers.

As long as he and Zoey want to rescue me, I'm the biggest liability in our entire operation.

JEMMA

Todd was ready to declare war on the Shadow Dynasty. Jemma tried pointing out to him repeatedly that, technically, they already had declared war the moment they stole some Whispers. But that didn't seem to be good enough for Todd. He wanted to skip the Knight Mares and go straight to the source. Cut off the head of the snake, he'd said.

That wasn't possible, though. No one even knew how to find the Shadow Dynasty outside of the Knight Mares, and they didn't even have an exact location for them. They just appeared to their soldiers when necessary and those soldiers were unlikely to let them ever get remotely close to the Dynasty. If they were to have any luck whatsoever at winning this war, they'd have to start at the bottom and work their way up.

They would also need a lot more manpower on their side. Best case scenario, they'd be able to rescue Zoey and, with her help, rescue others in her similar situation. Once they had enough people on their side who'd been able to break free from the Knight Mares, they could begin plotting out the best way to go on the offensive.

But first, they had to get Zoey. And to get Zoey, she had to get Todd to see the bigger picture. She was going to have to find a new way to approach him about it though, as her previous attempts had dissolved into unresolved arguments. Jemma watched as Todd paced back and forth in front of the giant map on the wall, looking at the pushpins they'd used to mark the few DNP locations they'd been able to locate.

By few, she meant five. In the whole world, they'd only found five locations. They knew generally where others might be, but until they could make contact with someone on the inside, they weren't precise. DNP's organization had operated underground, literally, for decades, maybe even centuries. No one even knew how long the Shadow Dynasty had existed.

"Todd, do you remember the year leading up to our wedding?"

"The year?" he stopped in his tracks, looking confounded as he pondered her question.

"Yes, the entire year. What do you remember about it?"

His brow furrowed as he tried to recall it.

"I remember it being a mostly normal year, Jemma. I was excited about getting married, and I remember we planned our honeymoon a few months before. But everything else was just life. We worked at different banks and saw each other when we could."

"And what do you remember about the actual wedding?"

"It was perfect. I remember how happy I was to see how happy you were, and it was the best moment of my life."

She smiled at her sweet, unsuspecting husband.

"Want to know what I remember about that year?"

"Uh, sure?"

"I remember working all day, every day, trying to rise up the corporate ladder then going home just to work more on the wedding. I remember months of looking for the perfect location, the most beautiful flowers, the best-fitting bridesmaid dresses. I remember agonizing over what song would play when. What kind and how much food we would feed the guests at the reception. I went through thirty different versions of invitations and wedding programs before settling on ones that went together just right. I hand glued over twenty thousand fake pearls to gold-leafed wine bottles to make centerpieces for all the tables. I tried on over three hundred dresses and spent months wondering if I'd made the wrong choice. Days before the wedding, I found out there'd been an accident at the place I took it for alterations and there were actual blood splatters on my train. I didn't know if I'd be able to wear the dress until about fourteen hours before the wedding."

"Why didn't you ever tell me about all of that? I could have helped."

"I wanted my magical wedding, Todd, and part of that was making sure it was magical for you too."

He stared at her in awe, and she smiled gently at him.

"The point is, we didn't just 'get married'. There was a lot of planning involved and lot of foundational pieces had to be laid first."

She waited as realization settled in on him.

"So, you're telling me to stop being stubborn and argumentative, and instead help you do all the hard work first?"

"Something like that."

"Fine, but Jemma?"

"Yes?"

"When we do finally go after the Shadow Dynasty directly, it's still going to be a magical day for both of us."

ZOEY

Zoey wasn't sure how much time had passed since the night the Director took over her mind. The Director had her on a set routine: get up, go to the gym, shower, sit in her room until he called for her, begrudgingly assist him as he tried to track down Jemma and Todd, return to her room (the best opportunity she had for writing messages to Doctor Sanderson), go to bed. He occasionally sprinkled meals in there, but he'd gotten pretty good at convincing her she wasn't hungry, despite the fight she still had in her.

She was getting weaker, though. It was increasingly difficult for her to push back against his thoughts and commands. Sometimes she even found it took a tremendous amount of weight off her to just go along with him. Doctor Sanderson continued to give her hope, though, and Zoey was determined that she would undo the Director and the entire Shadow Dynasty before she'd let herself be undone.

Sitting at her table with a notepad in front of her, she raised her left arm and brought her wrist down as hard as she could on the edge of the table.

Tell Jemma to move her team away from the Oregon hdqtrs. Board sending in massive Whisper and Knight Mare force.

She smashed her arm down on the table once again to remove any thought of the words she'd scrawled and shoved the note into her brace. Doctor Sanderson would always find a note there without her having to acknowledge it in any way. She blinked away tears as best she could, reeling from the battering of her arm. Apparently, she'd hit it with much more force than she'd initially intended.

What are you doing?

The voice in her head was angry, and she tried to think of her lie quickly enough that he couldn't tell she was processing her thoughts.

I got lightheaded and fell and landed on my arm.

That's it. Go to medtech right now and tell Doctor Sanderson I said to do whatever it takes to fix your wrist. I don't care if he has to tear off your entire arm, just get it done. Now.

That feels a little extreme.

ZOEY!

Yes, sir, I'm going.

For good measure, she rammed her arm into the wall as she was exiting her cabin.

Get it fixed, Zoey.

She managed a small smirk and a tiny speck of peace as she walked toward medtech and realized that the Director must have pulled back some to avoid the feeling of the throbbing assault on her arm. Now she just had to get that message to Doctor Sanderson, too.

DOCTOR SANDERSON

Doctor Sanderson grimaced as he took off Zoey's brace and realized what a mess her arm was. He read the note he found there, but quickly returned to examining her arm.

"We're definitely going to have to surgically repair this. You probably need a plate and screws."

He gingerly lifted her arm up, trying to avoid causing any additional pain at the moment. Their secret conversations could wait. He had a responsibility to her, after all, to take care of her.

"Okay." her voice was flat once again. He surveyed her carefully, more concern flooding into him. She was fading out to the point he almost couldn't recognize her anymore. He was going to have to push forward the timeline on getting her out of DNP and he resolved to discuss that with Jemma when he contacted her about the danger her team was facing.

He was also going to have to find a new way for communication with Zoey. Given the damage to her wrist, she was obviously going to greater lengths to hurt herself than he realized. If he didn't put a stop to it, she might cause permanent damage to it. He was furious with himself for suggesting she use such methods in the first place. Before he could say anything else, Zoey leaned forward and grabbed a pen from his shirt pocket, smashed her arm down on the bed rail, and scribbled a note as quickly as possible.

If the pain is unexpected and bad, he withdraws some.

He had to read the note twice. *She actually regained some control from him?* Now he was in an even worse situation. He absolutely could not allow Zoey to continue slamming her wrist against furniture. *But, if there really was a way to get him to voluntarily leave her, even just for a few moments...*

He held up a finger to her, indicating he would need a few minutes. Then, he used the phone on the wall to call the Director using the speakerphone function.

"What?" the Director snapped, and Doctor Sanderson could only assume he was reeling from the sudden impact.

"It's Doctor Sanderson. I can fix her wrist but it's worse than I initially thought. It looks like we missed something on the x-rays the first time. I'll have to surgically repair it using some metal hardware."

There was a pause that felt just a little too long.

"Fine. But don't fully sedate her. Use local anesthetics and pain killers. And keep her restrained while you do it, I don't want her trying to fight you because she can feel everything."

Sedation would solve that problem, though. And she won't be able to fight anyway unless...

Unless he can't access her at all if she's medically sedated. And unless he leaves her mind for the duration of the operation.

"Yes, sir. We'll be ready to operate first thing the day after tomorrow. I need some swelling to go down first. And it would be great if I could keep her here until then to try to keep her pain under control."

The Director gave a frustrated sigh on the other end of the line.

"Fine, but I am holding you to that timeline." and he hung up on Doctor Sanderson, who smiled as he began working out a plan in his mind.

DIRECTOR

Why hasn't she transformed yet?

"She's stronger than we could have imagined and she's still fighting against me. I can feel her getting weaker though, so it should only be a matter of time before she surrenders."

How much time?

"A week, maybe two, if that long at all. Her reluctance is slipping away the longer I'm in her mind."

If this works, she may be the strongest Knight Mare a Director has ever created. You've done good work. None of us believed the process would work if it wasn't voluntary.

"It will still be voluntary to some extent. She'll still have to make the choice to give up, anyway."

Regardless, we are impressed by your cunning plan of action. If the transformation is successful, you might have secured a place for yourself with us as a Shadow.

The Director bowed his head, feeling an overwhelming sense of pride and gratitude.

"I'm honored that you would even consider such an offer, and it is my pleasure to serve the Shadow Dynasty in any way you see fit."

Back at headquarters, the Director was alerted to an emergency in the wing where Trevor was being kept. Apparently, a staff member had gone into the cell to take what he believed was a sharp object. When he entered the cell, Trevor attacked him and was now holding him hostage, demanding the Director's presence. And Zoey's.

There was no chance the Director was taking Zoey into that environment, though. He had no idea what game Trevor was playing and there were far too many unknown variables. He could risk a resurgence in Zoey's memories of Trevor causing her will to strengthen. The Board would have his head if she wasn't transformed soon.

Angrily, he stalked through the building. He hated when people beneath him demanded that he do anything, and he'd already considered allowing Trevor to kill or maim the employee who'd stupidly gone in without backup in place. That would have been too difficult to explain to the majority of the staff who weren't knowingly involved in the work he was doing for the Board, though, so he fought through his disdain over the matter.

When he arrived, there were three security agents on the outside of the cell, weapons drawn and waiting for orders to move in on Trevor. The Director surveyed the situation.

"Leave us."

"Sir?" The security guard closest to him tore his gaze off Trevor and looked to the Director for confirmation of his order. The Director nodded.

"We'll be fine, won't we Trevor?"

"Yeah. We'll be fine. You heard him, get out of here." Trevor held the sharp object tighter against his hostage while the rest of the security team exited the area.

"How did you manage to get your hands on a weapon?" the Director asked coolly, trying to assess whether Trevor had anyone else on the inside helping him.

"I stole it, and that's as far as I'll go on that topic. You took her, didn't you? You stole Zoey."

The Director paused before answering, keenly aware that there was a witness to the conversation. *Trevor thinks I'll have no choice but to free him if we have this discussion in front of his prisoner.*

"Zoey is one of DNP's most valuable agents, Trevor. She is loyal to me, and to the Board. Unlike you, she has no ulterior motives for being here."

"She's not loyal to you anymore. That's why you took over her mind. I could see it in her eyes when you brought her here the other day. And where is she now? I said I wanted to speak to both of you."

"I don't typically stipulate to the ultimatums of traitors and prisoners. I'm here because you've placed a member of my team in harm's way, but I won't allow you to try to poison Zoey's mind with your incoherently rambled conspiracy theories."

"You're a liar. I know you're a Knight Mare. I know about the Shadow Dynasty. And I know that you've taken Zoey. Let her go, now. I'll kill him if you don't." Trevor's hands didn't shake a bit as he tightened his grip on his captive.

Well, that makes this easier for me.

"You have no idea what you've gotten yourself into here."

"I know exactly what I've gotten myself into, actually."

The Director flashed an evil grin at Trevor as he called upon his Whispers. In a moment, they'd encircled Trevor and forced him to stab his surety straight through the throat. The man crumpled to the floor, choking as he died. The Whispers yanked the scalpel out of his neck and the Director commanded them to secure Trevor against the back wall of his cell.

"Did Doctor Sanderson give this to you?"

"No."

"His death will be ten times more painful than yours if I find out you're lying to me again."

"He didn't give it to me. He was cleaning up the cut on my head and I managed to grab it from his bag while he wasn't looking."

"Good."

The Whispers wrapped around Trevor's mouth, forming a gag to muffle his screams, and the Director took his time slaying his foe.

DOCTOR SANDERSON

Time was of the essence. When they'd agreed to use Zoey's wrist surgery as a testing opportunity, they'd also agreed that they would have to make their final move to get the Director out of Zoey's head within the week. It was clear that she was not going to be able to hang on much longer and, without the ability to use the pain from her wrist anymore, it was nearly impossible to pass messages with her. Trevor's death made things even harder. The original plan had been for him to have an injury that needed treatment in the medical wing, then the two of them could work together to get Zoey out of the building. He may have been a tech guy, but he knew much more about how to handle the weapons Doctor Sanderson had gathered than he did. Now the only remaining options were to find a way to hurt Zoey so badly that the Director would be forced out and for the two of them to make a run for it before he could reestablish his connection (Jemma had calculated that they would need to be at outside of the building to keep him from reentering her mind without transforming back into his Knight Mare form), or Doctor Sanderson was going to have to fight his way out while dragging an unconscious agent along for the ride. Things weren't looking so great.

To make matters worse, the Director was keeping Zoey much closer to him for longer periods of the day. Jemma told Doctor Sanderson that was likely because he could feel her resolve weakening and was just waiting for the moment when she accepted the fate he was so determined to give her. That meant Doctor Sanderson was going to have to lure the Director away and get Zoey to medtech without the Director realizing something was going on. Secret operations were *not* part of his skill set.

As far as he could tell, Zoey still didn't know that Trevor was dead. The Director had instructed him not to discuss it with anyone under any circumstances, and he wouldn't even have conversations about Trevor and his "betrayal" around her, as if he feared discussing him at all in front of her. Doctor Sanderson was furious to find out that Trevor had stolen from him in order to enact his plan (which the Director described as a poorly thought-out escape attempt). If the Director had any question as to whether Doctor Sanderson had turned on him, he'd be dead too and there would be no hope for Zoey at all. For the life of him, he couldn't understand what Trevor was hoping to accomplish with his stunt but, whatever it was, Doctor Sanderson was convinced he'd failed.

More bad news I'll have to give her.

He took off his reading glasses and rubbed his eyes, closing the book that was hiding drawings of various exits around headquarters. Every possible route looked worse than the one before it but each time he got back to the start, he only found impossible options. He found himself longing for the day that this fight against the Shadow Dynasty was over once and for all, and he and all the others who'd taken up the cause could relax and enjoy life. Of course, he had no idea how long that might take, considering no one knew how many Knight Mares currently existed or how quickly new ones were being created. It was downright maddening and, for a brief moment, he wished he'd never gotten involved at all.

Guilt wracked him, though. So many people would need his medical assistance in this war. And he couldn't possibly regret all the lives that might be saved if the team could successfully save one life. Zoey's life. Determined to figure out the unsolvable puzzle of escaping the underground location, Doctor Sanderson put on his reading glasses and got back to analyzing each drawing once more.

By three in the morning, he'd narrowed down the seven possibilities to two, both of which were downright foolish as they required the doctor and Zoey to pass right in front of the Director's office. But they were also the only two options that deposited them into the parking garage. Doctor Sanderson figured that stealing a car would be the fastest way to get Zoey a safe distance away from the Director. He just had to figure out exactly *how* to steal a car and he woefully regretted his long-ago decision to not own a car or drive anywhere. He was sure to be rusty on a routine drive but in a high-speed chase, he was just as likely to kill himself and Zoey as he was to get them away.

A thought occurred to him, and he called Sarah, his medical assistant. She was home for the evening, one of the few employees who lived offsite, and would have to drive into work in the morning. He explained to her that he needed some additional supplies and asked if she would pick them up for him. He would reimburse her and help her bring them inside, she just needed to let him know when she arrived. That would give him the opportunity he needed to scope out the parking garage without arousing any suspicions.

Scope out the parking garage. If I fool myself into believing I'm as capable of this task as a real agent, I'll get us all killed.

It was the only logical plan he had though, so he resolved to go through with it. If nothing else, the excursion would show him just how hopeless their situation really was.

JEMMA

Doctor Sanderson informed Jemma that their escape plans would go into action the next morning. He'd also told her that Trevor was dead. She didn't buy the Director's story, either, but it hardly mattered at that point. Jemma and Todd would mourn the loss of their friend another time. For now, they had to figure out how to best position their resources for the extraction.

The tipoff Zoey had given Doctor Sanderson made a huge difference, and their team on Oregon had managed to clear out unscathed. A part of Jemma was sad to lose access to such valuable inside information, but she also knew that Zoey wouldn't be able to provide that for much longer anyway. If they couldn't save her tomorrow, they'd have to start treating her as the newest Knight Mare.

Jemma reflected on her own experience with the Shadow Dynasty, and how they'd tried to take hold of her and Todd. They had been able to withstand the Knight Mare's influence. The Dynasty had attempted to kill them as a result, but she and Todd had moved up so quickly in the banking world that their deaths would have left too many questions.

As far as she could tell, Zoey was much more strong-willed than she was, so she could only assume that the years Zoey spent living at DNP had contributed to the Director's ability to consume her mind. Doctor Sanderson had also mentioned that Zoey had been physically weak at that time, so she'd directed her team to do some research on the interplay between physical debility and a Knight Mare's ability to appropriate a mind. She'd almost felt stupid for even requesting the research when the answer came quickly: when one's physical being is subpar, one's mental wellbeing suffers. And if one's mental wellbeing is suffering, obviously one's mind would be easier to control.

She forced herself to return her thoughts to Doctor Sanderson's plans. No part of those plans seemed likely to succeed but, as he'd pointed out, no other options were really available to them. This made Trevor's reckless decision all the more infuriating to Jemma. After all, he could have at least waited until the escape attempt started to be a distraction to the Director. Jemma would have understood the sacrifice in that circumstance. As far as she could tell, though, Trevor had accepted the notion that he wouldn't survive the escape as the truth and chose to end things on his own terms. Of course, Doctor Sanderson had pointed out to her that Trevor's death had been fairly brutal, which meant his plans hadn't worked out quite the way he'd hoped they would.

A light touch on her shoulder ripped her from her thoughts, causing her to jump in her seat.

"I'm so sorry, Mrs. Maxwell. You weren't responding and I just wasn't sure you heard me."

"It's fine, Leann. I'm sorry, I didn't hear you though. What did you need?"

"We've got all the supplies ready in the medical wing to attend to Zoey tomorrow, and to Doctor Sanderson if he needs it. Also, Mr. Maxwell thinks he's found a Knight Mare working as an agent rather than a Director. If that's the case, then a lot more people are at the Shadow Dynasty's disposal than we initially thought."

"Thank you for working on the medical supplies. I'll go check in with Todd."

Jemma found Todd huddled over some paperwork in their strategic planning room, a far cry from the fancy offices they used to enjoy at the bank. Zoey's last day there had caused quite the storm for them and, with the ridiculous drug and kidnapping charges, they'd been forced to abandon their positions there. It had worked out well in the end, though, as they were able to give full-time focus to stopping the Dynasty.

"Leann mentioned something about a Knight Mare taking a lower role than Director?"

"Yeah. I'm starting to think the Dynasty ranks its Knight Mares sort of how the military ranks. You've got the Dynasty, then the "Directors," then it looks like there are Knight Mares who work as agents and turn people for the Dynasty while undercover. My guess is, once you've created enough Knight Mares, you get to rank up to Director. We found activity in Asia" he pointed to a glowing spot on the digital map, "indicating creation of a new Knight Mare, but there are no DNP headquarters in that area. So, we think a Knight Mare Director sent a Knight Mare Agent to recruit a new Knight Mare. If that's the case, it's hard to know whether all Knight Mares then join DNP under the local Director or if some Knight Mares just work independently. Either way, the Shadow Dynasty has a much bigger reach than we thought and it's going to take us much longer to bring them down. Zoey might be able to give us some insight but, at the end of the day, she's just the tip of the iceberg."

Overwhelmed, Jemma sank to the floor, sitting with her head in her hands.

"Should we stop this?"

"What?" Todd was incredulous.

"Do we stand a chance at ultimate success here? Can we even guarantee we can make a big enough dent in the system to make a difference? We aren't just risking our own lives by going after the Dynasty, Todd. So many people have followed us into this fight. I don't think I could live with myself if I knew I'd signed their death warrants just because I refused to acknowledge when we met our match."

Todd moved around the table and sat on the floor next to Jemma, gently draping an arm around her shoulders.

"They followed us because they agreed with us, Jemma. Everyone on our team knows how dangerous the Shadow Dynasty is but they still chose to be here. You haven't condemned anyone. You always want me to look at the details instead of the end game, so you should do that too. What's our first detail? We get Doctor Sanderson and Zoey out of DNP. That's our first battle and we can execute that plan. We'll worry about next steps when they come but every small victory we achieve hurts the Dynasty. We just have to keep picking the fights."

"And if we aren't successful tomorrow?"
"We will be."
"But if we're not?"
"Then we'll regroup and pick another fight."

DOCTOR SANDERSON

He awoke around 4:30 am, just a short time after he'd fallen asleep. Various meetings with Trevor somehow crept into his dreams, as if Trevor were urging him to recall some specific bit of information.

He took her to meet the Board.

That means Zoey had been in front of the Shadow Dynasty twice: once, shortly after Trevor was found out, and the second time when she realized what they really were. And if she'd gone to see them twice, he could only presume she'd met them in the same location. There was no indication that the Dynasty stayed close to their "boardroom," but if Zoey was able to give up its location, Jemma's team might be able to arrange a distraction. Surely, if the Dynasty were under direct attack, the local Knight Mares would be called upon to act as security. It did mean they would have to contend with more Knight Mares overall once they made their move but, just maybe, it would give them a small enough window to leave headquarters unnoticed.

He called Jemma immediately and couldn't help but notice the relief in her voice as she praised his idea. The biggest difficulty, they realized, would be getting the location from Zoey and then from

Doctor Sanderson to Jemma in the short span of the day. He was on his own in figuring that part out, but Jemma was already calling out to Todd in the background and telling him to get the team ready for an attack. Doctor Sanderson felt re-energized, as if there might actually be a chance that he and Zoey could get out of DNP alive. It wasn't much hope, but any hope was better than none at all.

There was zero chance of the Doctor going back to sleep after all the excitement he began getting ready for his day in medtech. Normally, he didn't have much to do during the days unless agents were returning from assignments that had gone wrong, but he also spent the entire day there anyway. The Director had grown accustomed to visiting him, it seemed, treating him as an old friend. He also liked to conduct research and perform experiments to determine new ways to help the agents he treated. It was a much better way to spend his days than sitting in his cabin waiting for someone to call on him.

Once in medtech, he began fidgeting about, reorganizing various parts of the unit while he waited for Sarah's call, his mind on ways to get to Zoey for the crucial information. When Sarah let him know she had arrived, he almost snapped at her for taking so long before realizing that it was only 8:30 am. His nerves were on edge and the stress was obviously getting to him, compounded with his underwhelming amount of sleep. Doctor Sanderson headed to the garage to meet her.

"What brings you all the way down here, Doc?" the Director called out as Doctor Sanderson passed his office.

"I've been researching methods for faster healing of wounds, and I asked Sarah to pick up some additional materials for me. I'm just on my way to help her bring them inside."

"I'll walk with you."

Good to see my plans are falling apart early.

"Are we still on track for Zoey's surgery in the morning? Her wrist seems to be giving her a lot of trouble."

"Yes, sir, it shouldn't be an issue." *Maybe this isn't all terrible after all!* "Actually, I'd be able to confirm it if she could stop by sometime this morning? I could see whether the swelling is actively decreasing and take one more round of images, so we have no holdups in the morning?"

"I'll send her your way when we come back inside. I think she'd really appreciate knowing that will all be handled soon."

If you're even allowing her to appreciate things.

"I must admit, I'm not very familiar with the parking garage so it may take me a moment to find where Sarah parked. . ."

"You've got a brilliant mind, Doc, but you're terrible with technology." The Director stepped through the door into the garage and tapped on a screen. A map of the garage showing each car on each level appeared. On the right-hand side was a touch keyboard. Doctor Sanderson watched as the Director tapped in Sarah's last name and a car on the screen lit up. Ground floor, around the corner from them.

"Well, isn't that just the most useful idea."

The Director chuckled at him the way Doctor Sanderson assumed children laughed at their grandparents.

"Do you need my help bringing your materials inside?"

"No, sir, I believe Sarah and I can manage. Thank you for...that." he waved his hand at the screen and gave his best, sympathetically lopsided smile.

"Zoey will be by to see you shortly." Doctor Sanderson watched for a moment as the Director walked back inside, then he made his way around the corner to Sarah.

ZOEY

Walking through headquarters, Zoey realized she'd felt compelled to visit medtech without ever hearing the Director's commands. It was almost as if their wills were merging into one. She tried briefly to make herself care but was unsuccessful. So, she continued toward medtech enjoying the silence in her head.

Doctor Sanderson looked up as the doors opened and she entered the room and they both stared at each other for a moment before he opted to break through the quietness.

"Zoey? Are you alright?"

Without saying a word, she plopped herself down in the chair next to him and robotically held out her left arm. When Doctor Sanderson didn't move, she spoke.

"I thought you needed to see my wrist."

She could barely hear herself talking, and that was a strange sensation. She noticed that everything around her sounded muffled and she frowned in response.

"Zoey?"

She heard her name, but just barely. Finally, it dawned on her that she was losing her fight with the Director but found herself utterly unable to mention it. Instead, Zoey just watched the physician as understanding settled in on him. Without warning, he grabbed a heavy binder and slammed it down on her arm. As affliction tore through her body, she was able to grasp onto a small piece of clarity, and she gasped in a deep breath.

"I can't hold him off any longer." she whispered her words, terrified the Director might hear her. Doctor Sanderson whispered back.

"You have to. Just until tomorrow, then I'm getting you out of here. You have to keep trying." He leaned forward, pressing the black binder down harder. "We don't have much time. I need you to tell me where the Boardroom is and what security is like there."

"Why would you need that? We can't go there; we'd never make it out alive."

"I can't give you any more details than that, Zoey. He's too entwined in your thoughts. Please, just tell me and I'll explain when we're gone tomorrow."

As the pain began to subside, her sense of emptiness returned. Zoey's demeanor changed back into the flatness she'd had when she first entered medtech.

"Swelling. . . x-ray. . ." she murmured, her eyes unfocused. She was aware that Doctor Sanderson was moving, but she stayed still in her chair. A new sensation flowed through her arm, grabbing her attention enough for her to realize the doctor was trying gently to remove the brace from her wrist. He was saying something about the amount of damage to it, but her thoughts were on nothing at all.

Nothing, that was, until her eyes found a report of death on the backside of his desk that had a familiar name written at the top.

"Trevor..."

The name sounded funny as it fell from her mouth. Immediately, the Director was in her mind.

What did you say?

Trevor. I know someone named Trevor.

No. You don't.

I think...I think I do.

You didn't really know him. He was a traitor. He wanted you dead.

Oh...he...drugged me?

Yes, that's right. And he wanted to take you away from me. But you didn't want to go.

I didn't want to go?

"Zoey? Zoey, can you hear me?"

I wanted...something.

You wanted to stay with me. You wanted the Board to promote you.

No.

Zoey.

No, I wanted you out of my head. I still want you out of my head.

Stop it.

Get out.

Listen to me.

Get out.

I'm not going anywhere, Zoey, so stop trying to fight me. We are so close to being through with this.

"GET OUT!" She screamed the words as loud as she could before slumping forward in her chair. Zoey had spent every ounce of energy she'd been able to muster, but there was no way she could force him completely from her mind. Doctor Sanderson kneeled in front of her, worry etched along his face, as he checked to see if she was alright.

"Do it again so I can tell you about the Boardroom." she said, jabbing at her arm.

DIRECTOR

Throwing his cell phone across his office in frustration, the Director stood and paced while trying to get a hold on his anger as Zoey's flashes of pain continued to attack him. He couldn't very well burst into medtech to handle the situation. Doctor Sanderson would have too many questions and the Director needed to keep the physician as aligned with his perception of DNP's purpose as possible.

He'd been in such a good mood that morning, too. Normally he never would have offered to walk with the doctor to the parking garage and made small talk. But he'd known from the moment she woke up that Zoey was giving up. The Director had been on the verge of ultimate victory. Somehow, she broke through it. He wasn't even sure what had triggered the memories of Trevor in her mind. He'd tried looking through her immediate memories but all he'd been able to find was the recurring trauma from her injury. He gave brief consideration to ordering Doctor Sanderson to perform her surgery immediately, but he still had his cover to maintain.

For a moment, he wondered whether fixing her wrist was actually a bad idea. Perhaps it had been the constant pain that helped break her down.

Regardless, she was too weak to fight him off anymore anyway. He sensed that during their argument just a moment ago. She'd summoned an extreme amount of energy just to argue with him inside her head and, from what he could tell, screaming the words "get out" had been completely debilitating. Zoey would be ready to begin her transition into a Knight Mare in a matter of days and become an unstoppable force for the Board, and his reward would soon follow.

Feeling Zoey's pain starting up again, he withdrew from her mind once more. The Director could leave and reenter it at will and he didn't see the point in allowing her agony to infiltrate him. Since she'd used all her energy reserves to yell at him, he saw no potential risks. It was nice to have some quiet back in his own mind, no longer sharing a space with a girl who'd grown to hate him in such a short amount of time. He knew she'd come around once this battle was over, but in the meantime, it felt nice to not be engaged in mental warfare with someone who wished him dead several times a day. He was also glad for a moment to work without having to block his thoughts off from her. Zoey wasn't nearly powerful enough to use their entanglement against him, but there was always the possibility that he might accidentally let a wall down himself. Until she was ready for her transformation, it seemed best to keep her knowledge of DNP's missions on a strict need-to-know basis.

Somehow, the Maxwells had been tipped off and their team in Oregon had managed to pull out before the group of Knight Mares the Dynasty sent in were able to corner them. The general consensus was that there had to be a leak in one of the DNP locations in that area, but none of the Directors had been able to root out the source yet. He hadn't let himself believe they would have captured Jemma and Todd during that mission, but he had hoped that those Knight Mares could have at least taken enough hostages to get some usable information. Instead they were back to the drawing board, trying to determine where the next attempted insurgence might occur.

He continued working, plotting out weaknesses in DNP's defenses, and calling other Directors to offer assistance where he could, all the while remaining pulled back from Zoey's mind while she was with Doctor Sanderson. Everything was safe as long as she was there in medtech, after all.

ZOEY

Zoey blinked back tears as she used a tape dispenser to pound the same spot on her leg over and over in an attempt to use that pain to keep the Director from overhearing her conversation with Doctor Sanderson. He'd flat-out refused to let her do any more damage to her wrist and was cautiously inspecting it while they spoke. She'd given him as much information as she could remember about the boardroom, including a rough drawing of the interior floor plan. As much of it as she'd seen, anyway. Zoey knew there was at least a second floor in the building, but had no idea how it was laid out or what its purpose was generally.

Once she'd given up as much information about the boardroom as she could, Zoey and Doctor Sanderson began plotting out their escape attempt. At that time, Doctor Sanderson explained Trevor's death to her, and Zoey was at a loss. She'd been so mad at him before she realized the truth about the Director and the Board, and she'd never gotten a chance to apologize to him. She also couldn't fathom why he'd taken the action he had when he did. Something felt off about the whole situation. Zoey didn't have time to dwell on either her sadness or her confusion, though, and she tried to maintain concentration on keeping Doctor Sanderson alive the next morning when he would risk everything to help her get away from DNP.

In a perfect world, the Director would rush to the boardroom and take his best agents with him under the guise of protecting the Board. They considered that he might halt her procedure and demand she rush off with him, though, which would cause a breakdown of the entire plan. Doctor Sanderson was going to have to make sure Jemma was able to hold her team back until he actually opened up Zoey's wrist. That changed their plans, too, because they'd initially planned to wait until Zoey was safely away from DNP before performing the actual procedure.

So, Doctor Sanderson would open up her wrist as little as possible to ensure that the Director would leave without Zoey. Once the DNP headquarters was cleared out as much as possible, they would slip out to the parking garage. The doctor would maintain enough pressure on Zoey's wrist to keep the pain steady without causing too much additional harm to it so that the Director wouldn't be tempted to reenter her mind before they'd exited. Fortunately, they would be traveling in the opposite direction from the boardroom, so they should be able to create enough distance to keep him from reasserting his control over her. Zoey had to convince him that their best chance of escape was for him to steal Sarah's car keys, since they already knew how to find her car and it would be easy to get to. Doctor

Sanderson was horrified by the idea of stealing from her, but Zoey explained that was just an unfortunate byproduct of working in covert operations. He'd argued that he was a doctor and not an agent, but quieted his protests once Zoey pointed out he'd voluntarily joined the Maxwells in their cause and that he was the one who first assisted Zoey in communicating without the Director overhearing.

When they finally recognized that they'd talked the plan over as much as they possibly could, they decided to call it a day. Zoey was worried about how easy the whole plan sounded given the Director's otherworldly abilities, but as long as he didn't insist she go with him to defend the Board, there was no reason to believe things wouldn't go as they hoped. She waited dutifully while Doctor Sanderson called the Director to let him know they were finished and was relieved that the Director ordered her to return to her cabin and take it easy until the surgery could be completed. No doubt that was for his own benefit, but Zoey was happy enough to not be dragged into a conference room to help plan attacks on the people trying to save her.

DOCTOR SANDERSON

The last time Doctor Sanderson felt as nervous as he was the day of the planned escape was when he was still in medical school and he was performing his first surgery. Even then, he'd been pretty confident in his abilities and studies. This was different. Zoey had tried to reassure him several times while they were planning the night before, but he could tell she wasn't entirely convinced of their potential for success either. He had to stay as positive about it as possible, though. Zoey had explained that stress and nerves lead to bigger mistakes in the field, which he knew to some degree, but he'd never before considered how difficult the typical DNP agent's job was and found himself worrying about all those people he and Zoey were leaving behind on top of his fear of not surviving the day.

He waited impatiently for both Zoey and Sarah. Originally, he was supposed to steal Sarah's keys before Zoey even arrived; however, he was concerned he might need backup or a diversion as he'd never actually stolen anything before. In his mind, it was a miracle Zoey hadn't ridiculed him. Instead, she listened patiently and then offered up the idea of waiting until she had gotten there just in case.

Somewhat surprisingly, Zoey arrived before Sarah. *The Director must really want her arm fixed quickly.* He made small talk with her, asking about how she was feeling and if she'd slept well that night. He didn't bother asking her if she'd been eating lately. It was obvious from her unhealthy appearance that it was not a priority in the Director's mind. He supposed it helped the Director maintain a tighter grip on her mind.

I've got to get this girl away from here. Not just to save her mind, but to save her physical health too.

Zoey gave very brief responses to his questions and even the effort of her monosyllabic retorts affected her. He watched as she struggled for a moment to even sit upright in a chair before giving up and leaning backwards into it, as though she'd fall straight to the floor if it wasn't there to prop her up.

At least I don't have to worry about her thoughts giving our plans away. I doubt there's anything going through her mind at all right now.

It was at that moment he realized Zoey would be of no help to him in pilfering Sarah's keys. She certainly couldn't steal them herself and she wasn't physically or mentally capable of causing a scene. The only way she could help is if he hurt her somehow first but, given the forthcoming events, he couldn't quite bring himself to start the party so early. So, he set about helping Zoey stand and moving her to the bed where he would begin the surgical procedure. When she was all squared away, he began preparing the tools he would need until Sarah got to work.

This would be the morning she's not here early.

The medtech phone rang, and he knew who it was before answering.

"Medtech, this is Doctor Sanderson."

"Has Zoey made it there yet?"

"Yes, sir. She's here. I'm just getting everything ready so I can start just as soon as Sarah makes it in this morning."

"Call me the second you're finished. I want this wrapped up as fast as you can do it."

"Of course, Director."

Shortly after the call ended, Sarah appeared in medtech, looking frazzled. Doctor Sanderson's heart dropped from his chest as she detailed the accident she'd had on her way to work after her front left tire blew out on the highway. While Sarah continued telling her story, he began feeling as though he were trying to listen to her from underwater, and sweat beads formed on his head.

This is it. This one thing is going to ruin our whole plan before we even get started. I built every bit of my hope on the presumed reliability of someone else's vehicle. I'm an absolute fool. Jemma needs to know that we have to call this off because there's no way we can just find someone's keys and car quickly enough to get away. Why did I never give in and buy my own car? Zoey's going to be lost forever and this will all be my fault because I believed I could be the Maxwells' inside guy, despite my utter lack of skills in anything other than practicing medicine. I've doomed us all. I've doomed-

"Doc? Doc, are you feeling alright?"

Concern filled Sarah's eyes as they searched his face for an answer.

"What?"

"Are you okay? You just sort of zoned out for a minute there."

"Uh...yes, yes I'm fine. Just worried about you, you know."

"Oh, well, like I was saying, no one got hurt and I was able to put the spare tire on to get here. Someone's supposed to be coming this afternoon to tow it to a shop to replace the tire completely."

I'm retiring the very second we are safely away from this place.

"Great!" he said a bit too enthusiastically. "Great, that's just, that's great news. Hey, why don't you leave your keys on the counter and I'll have Zoey take a look at it after we fix up her wrist. She might be able to give you some insight before you go so they don't try to oversell you or anything."

There's absolutely no way that is going to work. Sarah is far too intelligent to fall for such a stupid line-

"Do you really think she would do that? I'd appreciate it so much, I don't know anything about cars!"

Everything I know is wrong.

"Sure, I'll talk to her about it." "Thanks, Doctor! That will really take some stress off me today."

Instead of setting her keys down on the desk, she plopped them directly into his hand, not a concern in her mind. He smiled at her as he stuck them in his pocket and turned away to head into the small surgical room where Zoey was waiting.

JEMMA

Much to Todd's chagrin, Jemma refused to send team members to the boardroom without going herself. He'd wanted her to stay safely behind. He told her that she was too valuable to the overall mission and everything would fall apart if something happened to her. She supposed there might have been some truth in that, but she knew he really wanted her to stay behind because he was worried about her. At the end of the day, she felt the same about him but she wouldn't ask him to stay behind. As much as they cared for each other, they were also all-in on today's mission. No one really expected them to do much damage to the Shadow Dynasty but, if they were lucky, they could contain enough Whispers to take down a few Knight Mares and save Zoey and Doctor Sanderson while they were at it. At the very least, they hoped they could incapacitate the Director. That alone would be a huge blow to the Dynasty's local operations.

The longer they waited for Doctor Sanderson's signal, the more antsy she got. They hadn't been able to settle on an exact start time for this operation; instead, they'd had to work out a window of possibility. Nothing could happen until Doctor Sanderson cut into Zoey's wrist and, even then, he would have to be able to notify Jemma that it was time to move. If the Director decided to be present for the procedure, they would have to call the whole thing off before making any moves.

She bounced her leg up and down rapidly as she sat in the car waiting for time to move. On top of the general risk associated with their pending attack, Jemma and Todd had to stay out of public view as much as possible. Their reputations were still in the mud after news reports labeled them as drug dealers who'd probably been trying to pull Katie Charles into a human trafficking ring. She couldn't wait to make the Director pay for that garbage spin.

Jemma felt a small vibration on her wrist and looked down at her smart watch to see a text message from Doctor Sanderson:

Wrist open. Director not in here. Go.

A buzz of electrical energy filled Jemma's body as she grabbed a hand radio and announced all teams were a go. She and Todd jumped out of their car and raced toward the Boardroom with the rest of the volunteers on their side. As quickly as possible they hit security guards with tranquilizer darts and worked to set up as many of their Whisper-catching machines as possible. All in, they had seven in place before they heard an alarm sound. She looked to Todd, who nodded his head at her as she spoke.

"This is it. We're in it now."

DIRECTOR

The Director sat back, relaxed in his chair, enjoying a cup of coffee. He'd relinquished control of Zoey's mind when Doctor Sanderson told him the surgery was starting and was glad he didn't have to deal with Zoey's reactions to the physical pain. He was also glad that he'd finally won the battle for her mind. Before the surgery started, she thought of literally nothing. He had free rein over her thoughts and she no longer had the ability to contemplate anything he didn't directly put into her mind. Once her procedure was finished, he planned to take her back to the Board to initiate the transformation process. She would belong to him forever.

A red light on the wall to his right began flashing and a monitor lit up below it. A message ran across the screen telling him the Boardroom was under attack and a camera feed showed him several security guard members on the ground while a group of people in street clothes took defensive positions within the building. He hastily placed down his mug, sploshing some coffee out onto his desk, and reached for his office phone to call in all available agents to defend the Board. His next thought was to get Zoey, but he knew there was no way that the doctor would let her go anywhere until he'd finished placing the plates and screws in her arm. The timing was awful, but it was unlikely the group attacking the Boardroom had the resources to fight both a team of trained agents and a Knight Mare or two. He called and ordered transport to get ready to take him to the Boardroom and he rushed through the halls grabbing each capable-looking person he could on his way to the garage.

His driver sped off as soon as the Director made it to his SUV. He couldn't comprehend how any rational person could think he or she could take down the Board, but he also couldn't understand how these people knew where the Boardroom was at all. There'd been a severe breach somewhere, and he could only hope it hadn't come from within his team. That wasn't something the Board seemed likely to forgive.

Despite the fact that almost none of DNP's agents had been to the Boardroom before, they'd all been taught defense protocol in case something like this ever happened using a mock building at headquarters. Fortunately, that meant he didn't have to do anything more than order Protectorate Protocol to get everyone on his command moving to take back the Boardroom. Looking around, he noticed the Maxwells off to the side yelling orders to their people.

This is how they are trying to draw Zoey out. They wanted me to bring her so they could try to take her from me.

The thought infuriated him and, without further consideration, he moved toward them. When he was only a few steps away, a flash of light blinded him and Whispers began seeping out of his disguise and hurtling toward a contraption on the ground, which he recognized based on a previous description as the one used on another Knight Mare days before. His anger had led him directly into one of their traps. Despite the absence of his Whispers, though, he still felt strong enough to take action against the Maxwells. He hadn't become a Director by acting recklessly, though, so he stopped his movements and acted as though their first round assault on him did significantly more damage than it had.

"So it's true. You've figured out how to take Whispers."

"Yeah, and now you're nothing without them." Todd stepped forward slightly, boasting at their ingenuity.

So brash. I'm going to enjoy destroying him, too.

"Where's Zoey?" Jemma spoke up, worry etched on her face as she maintained the healthy distance away from him.

"That's none of your concern, Mrs. Maxwell." he stumbled slightly to add a bit of dramatic flair.

"You've stolen the life of a bright young woman and we want her back."

"Interesting. During the entire time you knew her, she was working against you. Yet here you are, risking the lives of so many" he gestured at all the volunteers around the building, backing themselves into the walls as more Knight Mares began appearing, "just to rescue a girl who doesn't need or want it."

"Take their Whispers!" Todd yelled at the others as the reinforcement Knight Mares got closer and a flurry of flashes brought them to their knees as their Whispers were stolen.

Interesting. Some of us are weaker without Whispers than others.

"It's not up to you whether she needs or wants help." Todd's words were angry, and he stalked closer to the Director.

"At this point in time, yes, I believe it is."

"Todd, come back. Director, release Zoey or our team will move onto the next phase of our plan."

He laughed. *She's threatening* me? *This woman is as headstrong as Zoey used to be. No wonder the Board wanted her to join the Knight Mares.*

"Mrs. Maxwell, how much do you really know about my abilities? *Our* abilities?"

"Enough to know you're poisoning that girl."

"Enough to know I can control more than one mind at a time?"

In that moment, it felt like the world stopped. The Director watched as the Maxwells' eyes enlarged in real time and they began grasping the meaning of what he'd just said. The sound around them fell away and, in the speediest of movements, he dropped his disguise and took his Knight Mare form, rushing full force into Todd's mind.

ZOEY

In a daze, Zoey allowed Doctor Sanderson to drag her through medtech, listening as he ordered Sarah to take cover in case the attack on the Boardroom came for headquarters. Zoey knew that wasn't going to happen but was impressed by how convincing the doctor's concern had been anyway. She was a little woozy from the feeling of Doctor Sanderson slicing her arm open without so much as a hint that it was coming but was still surprised when he easily manipulated her so that she was pressed face first into the wall.

"Hold still." his voice was gruff as he lifted her shirt in the back. She struggled to fight him off, unsure of what he was doing, when he tightened his hold. He slid a metal disc along her back and then she felt a sharp twinge.

"Let me go." she weakly protested.

"Stop moving or this isn't going to work." He leaned his shoulder into her a little harder, and she felt the interrogation chip get sucked out of her back. It hurt worse than when he removed the GPS tracker, but she assumed the chip must have been a little bigger to cause the havoc that it did.

"Hey, I thought you couldn't do that..." she started slipping down the wall, no strength left to hold herself upright.

"He lied. About everything, Zoey, he lied to you."

"That's what Trevor said. Wait, we have to get Trevor," she tried to pull her arm away from Doctor Sanderson after he'd hoisted her back to her feet, but he pulled her along with him toward the parking garage. Zoey walked with him for a moment before telling him they messed up their plans by not working out an escape for Trevor too.

"Zoey, you saw the paperwork in my office yesterday. Remember? You had a fight with the Director. Trevor's dead. We have to get out of here."

"Dead. Dead...how did he die?" she stopped, planting herself as firmly as she could while she waited for a satisfactory answer.

"The Director killed him, Zoey, let's go. We have to go."

She saw it clearly in her mind, as if she were the Director. She watched as Trevor tried in vain to negotiate, using the life of a staff member as a pawn. She heard as he demanded the Director leave her alone and she felt herself watching with a twisted joy as Trevor was horrifically murdered. And she felt a rage swell in her as she came to the conclusion that the Director had to die for all the things he'd done. He had to die.

Today.

DIRECTOR

Todd's resistance to the Director's control was unimpressive. Within seconds of entering his mind, the Director gained full control of Todd, and Todd's protests weren't much more than hushed pleas. In a full display of his strength despite lacking his Whispers, the Director took full possession of Todd's body and lunged at Jemma. He tackled her to the ground and placed both hands tightly around her throat.

"Todd," she gasped, struggling to catch her breath, "Todd, if you can hear me-"

He strengthened his grip.

"You have to-have-have to fight him."

This time he tightened his hold on her so much that she could no longer speak at all, and watched with glee as she tried to grapple with him, her eyes bulging as her face turned purple. Then, just before she died, he pulled himself from Todd's mind and body and entered Jemma's.

He sat up, breathing hard, as he watched Todd fall to the ground with tears in his eyes. The Director stood and moved toward Todd, but Jemma had more fight in her. She pulled back before he could make contact.

Leave him alone. Leave me alone.

You were stupid to think you could fight me here today. Even if I'd brought Zoey, none of you would have made it out alive. She would have seen to that for me.

Get out of my head.

Unlock my Whispers.

You know I won't.

Do I know that?

You do now.

Todd. Todd, it's me, it's Jemma, you have to unlock the Whispers.

STOP! Don't use my voice, you monster, stop!

Todd, he'll kill me. Please save me.

I'm going, Jemma. Just hold on a little longer.

Todd, NO! He's controlling us both, that's why you think you hear me.

But I do hear you.

Leave us, now!

Todd, if you don't release the Whispers, Jemma will die.

Don't hurt her. I'll do anything, just don't...

Stop listening to him, Todd.

But it was too late. Todd had released the Director's Whispers and told everyone else to release theirs as well. They rushed to their various masters, ready to do their bidding. The Director's Whispers told the other that they could have everyone else but that Jemma and Todd were his. Then he used his Whispers to hold them still as every single volunteer on their team was destroyed.

He took back his human form but remained within Jemma's head.

You'll never take her from me, Jemma.

I already have.

The Director cocked his head to the side.

"What do you mean by that?"

"I mean she's already left DNP headquarters and is safely away from you."

Kill Todd.

No.

Fine, but it's going to be worse if I do it.

Leave him alone. You've lost her. And you'll lose this war.

He felt out for Zoey's mind and found that he could still talk to her.

Where are you, Zoey?

None of your business.

He could tell by her tone she was angry, but he couldn't feel it.

Come to me.

Oh I'm going to come for you. And I'm going to kill you.

Outraged at the loss of power over his prized recruit, the Director snapped his fingers and his Whispers snapped Todd's neck. His blazing eyes found Jemma's, who was still restrained by the Whispers.

"I'll just have to settle for you instead."

DOCTOR SANDERSON

He'd never been more thankful for anything than he was that he'd had the foresight to grab a sedative shot in case he needed it during the escape. The second Zoey relived Trevor's death through the Director's memory, she'd gone on a rampage. Then, when she realized they could still speak to each other through their bizarre mental connection, she began taunting him. This girl had been to hell and back and her body was literally giving out on her, and yet she still found a sliver of fight within herself and drew on it.

They almost wrecked when he jabbed the syringe into her neck and he'd been just barely able to take control of Sarah's car. After a few minutes of driving, he pulled over in a secluded lot and stepped out of the car. He had been sitting in Zoey's lap to drive and needed to make sure she wasn't injured any more than she already had been. When he was convinced that she was mostly okay, he wrestled her into the passenger's seat and placed the safety buckle around her, then got back in himself to drive to the rendezvous point.

Doctor Sanderson grew more nervous with each bump in the road, praying that the spare tire would hold out just long enough to deliver them to safety. He also hadn't heard back from Jemma or anyone else on the team, and was growing increasingly anxious to meet up with everyone. Finally, he found the closed road he'd been instructed to follow. It took him deep into the woods where a makeshift road had been cleared before leading out to a building that looked much like an abandoned factory. The doctor presented his ID to a guard, who directed him further down the path to a smaller building being used for medical care. Several others met him there and helped him pull Zoey from the car so that he could finally set about healing the broken young woman.

ZOEY

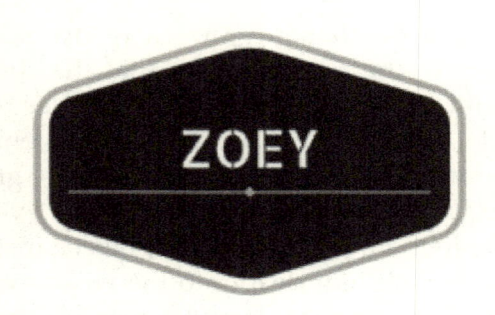

Groggily, Zoey opened her eyes and struggled to take in her new surroundings. Her eyes acknowledge the solid cast on her left arm, along with an IV in her right arm. Discomfort on her face led her to the realization that a feeding tube had been inserted through her nose. She thought it a bit of an extreme measure and wanted to remove it, but Doctor Sanderson noticed her movements and scolded her for even thinking about it.

"How did it go? Have Jemma and Todd made it back?" her voice was weak, but she finally sounded like herself again, which gave her some relief.

"It…didn't go very well." She watched as he avoided making eye contact with her.

"How bad was it?"

"You don't need to worry about it right now. Try to rest up and then we can talk about it."

"I'm not going to rest until I at least know what's going on, so just tell me."

Doctor Sanderson sighed.

"We lost them."

"The whole team?" She caught his hesitation. "What happened, Doc?"

"One team member came back alive. The Knight Mares killed basically everyone else."

"Basically? What are you leaving out?"

"Please, Zoey, now isn't the time-"

"Tell me." Her voice grew stronger with the command.

"The Director...he took over Jemma and Todd's minds the way he did yours. He killed Todd, but he still has Jemma."

Zoey felt like she was going to be sick. All of that planning and fighting to free her, and the Director just took Jemma instead. He would kill her; there was no doubt in Zoey's mind.

"We have to go back for her."

"And we will, but we have to regroup first. We lost a lot of our volunteers at the Boardroom."

"I should have never told you how to get there. They never stood a chance."

"They knew the risk they were taking. And we learned some things in the process. Most Knight Mares can't function without their Whispers, but the Director can. That's important information to have before we try to go after him again."

"*We* aren't going after him again. I'm going to go after him, and I'm going to end this."

"I know you have a score to settle here, but you have to remember something: you're not the only victim. There's a whole world full of people who have gone through or are going through exactly what just happened to you. We have to help at least some of them first or we'll never have the resources to save them all."

Zoey pressed her head back into her pillow, a migraine forming. She knew he was right, but that didn't help contain her fury. In that moment, she knew she would do whatever it took to not only free Jemma, but to see her vision come true.

JEMMA

As the darkness around her cleared and her mind cleared, Jemma took in her surroundings. She was in a small room she assumed DNP used for interrogations.

You catch on quickly.
I told you to get out of my head.
Sit down.

Against her will, her body moved to a chair in the corner of the room and sat. Jemma opened her mouth to speak but was unable to do so.

I won't let you win. You won't break me.

I already broke you. Todd is dead. You're here, and you can't fight me. I've learned from my mistakes with Zoey. There's no way out of this for you. The Dynasty will love having you finally join them.

I will never join them. I'll never be on your side.

Never is a very long time, Jemma. I'm interested to see how long you really make it before giving into me.

The next thing she knew, she was writhing on the floor, screaming in anguish. Tears forced themselves from her eyes and she gasped hard for breath. When it stopped, the Director spoke over a microphone into the room.

"I don't think it will take very long at all."

ZOEY **DIRECTOR**

You knew someone had to take your place, right? Because of your selfishness, you've condemned Jemma to live in this life that you say isn't worth living, that's no good for anyone.

I'll come back and free her.

Then what, Zoey? There will be another and another and another. The cycle will always continue.

I'll come back then, again and again and again, as many times as I have to in order to stop you.

You know only the Board can stop me, Zoey. Even if I wanted to, I could never quit unless they allowed it.

Then I'll stop the Board. I'll go after each and every member until no one else is trapped so alone and in despair.

And I'll be nothing to you despite all the years I gave you, despite how I provided for you.

Things you wouldn't have had to do if you hadn't killed my parents.

They never would have loved you or cared for you the way I have.

Well, I'll never get the chance to know for sure, will I? Because of you.

We need each other.

We did. And maybe you still need me. But I don't need you anymore.

Even if I can't control you, I'll always be in your mind. You'll always be able to hear my voice.

That doesn't mean I have to listen.

Made in the USA
Coppell, TX
17 July 2022